21 FANTASTIC FAILURES

Sonali Misra decided at a young age that if she was ever going to be stuck working at a desk, it would be for something she enjoyed. She mapped out her life accordingly (or at least she likes to think so), so that it would revolve around her passion for words and stories. She began writing at the age of eight and has now been published in British and Indian anthologies, and of course, the book you're holding.

Born and brought up in Delhi, Sonali attained her Bachelor's in English from Lady Shri Ram College for Women, worked in book publishing for four years and then completed a Master's degree in creative writing from The University of Edinburgh, United Kingdom. While in the UK, she also co-founded an international literary magazine that exclusively promotes underrepresented voices. She is currently pursuing her PhD in Publishing Studies from the University of Stirling, UK, and is simultaneously working on her first novel.

Twitter @MisraSonali | www.sonalimisra.com

21

FANTASTIC

FAILURES

and what their stories teach us

SONALI MISRA

RUPA

Published by
Rupa Publications India Pvt. Ltd 2020
7/16, Ansari Road, Daryaganj
New Delhi 110002

Sales centres:
Allahabad Bengaluru Chennai
Hyderabad Jaipur Kathmandu
Kolkata Mumbai

ISBN: 978-93-89967-51-7

First impression 2020

10 9 8 7 6 5 4 3 2 1

The moral right of the author has been asserted.

Printed at HT Media Ltd, Noida

For my parents:
Thank you for allowing me to fail,
yet always believing I would rise.

CONTENTS

Introduction   *ix*

Struggles Are Inevitable   1
    Amitabh Bachchan: Bollywood actor

Adapt, or Become Irrelevant   10
    Steve Jobs: Co-founder of Apple Inc.

We Are Not Our Circumstances   19
    Oprah Winfrey: TV personality

How We Play Counts More Than Winning   28
    Lionel Messi: Footballer

Say Yes to Smart Risks   36
    Richard Branson: Co-founder of Virgin Group

Find Joy in Work   45
    Vincent van Gogh: Painter

Nothing Can Replace Hard Work and Perseverance   53
    Thomas Edison: Inventor

Do Not Fear Failure   62
    Julia Child: Cookbook author and TV personality

No Work Is Small Work   70
    Dr. Seuss: Children's author

Success Requires Sacrifice   79
    Nelson Mandela: Political activist and
    former President of South Africa

It's Never Too Late   88
   Colonel Sanders: Founder of KFC

Challenges Reveal Our Best Selves   97
   Elon Musk: Founder of SpaceX and Co-founder of Tesla

Focus on the Big Picture   106
   Serena Williams: Tennis player

Harness Every Teammate's Strength   114
   Walt Disney: Co-founder of The Walt Disney Company

Choose Inspiration Over Comparison   124
   Albert Einstein: Physicist

Remain Flexible for Reinvention   133
   Vera Wang: Fashion designer

Critics Aren't Always Right   141
   The Beatles: Band

Master Trades Relevant to the Job   150
   Michael Jordan: Basketball player

More Than One Route Leads to Triumph   158
   Steven Spielberg: Hollywood director and producer

Prosperity Does Not Equal Success   166
   Ratan Tata: Chairman of Tata Trusts and
   former Chairman of Tata Sons

Be Kind to the Self   174
   Lady Gaga: Musician

Acknowledgements   184

INTRODUCTION

As children, we read fairy tales and fables that preach morals we should abide by—'unity is strength', 'a bird in hand is worth two in the bush', 'do unto others as you would have them do unto you'. But as we grow older and experience the complexities of life, these lessons seem simplistic and the stories they've been derived from too idealistic. How are we supposed to empathize with farmyard animals and princes and princesses in these stories for children, when we believe adulthood problems aren't as straightforward? We need *real* incidents we can relate to from the lives of actual people who have walked on our earth and encountered things we do on a daily basis. Where are our real-life heroes—the ones we can look up to and learn from?

The aim of *21 Fantastic Failures (and What Their Stories Teach Us)* is precisely this. Presented in this book are the lives of 21 legends from various fields—business, science, technology, politics, sports, literature, art, film, TV and music, from India and abroad—in easy-to-read short chapters. These notable individuals, living or dead, are already known to most of us, even if in various degrees of familiarity; perhaps, we've heard of them as pioneers of their fields or maybe we're ardent followers of their work. The one thing they all have in common is that they *failed*. They failed in either their personal or professional struggles, as we all do. However, what sets them apart is that they actively chose to not let those obstacles stop them from achieving what they had set their minds to. Ultimately, they will live on in history books as luminaries who contributed to their respective domains and left a mark on this world.

WHY FAILURES?

Why look at people who have failed though? Why not idolize those who achieved everything they ever wanted to, and aspire to those standards of being? Shouldn't we aim for perfection anyway?

But therein lies the problem—study any well-known person closely enough, and we'll find cracks in the veneer. Nobody is perfect, and everyone struggles in ways we sometimes cannot imagine. It is perhaps the one thing that binds us all—we dream and desire, and we work towards fulfilling them, but our paths are ridden with hurdles. How we choose to react to those hindrances sets the tone for what our futures may hold.

This may all sound grand, maybe even a bit grandiose. What if our lives are headed in the direction we have always wanted and we don't need to refer to anyone else's life story? That's exactly where the beauty of the Lasting Lessons lies. They are simple enough to be applied day-to-day, and not just in the professional sphere, but also at home, school or within our social network. These little nuggets ensure we play, *and play well*, the game of life and the googlies it throws at us.

HOW DOES THIS BOOK WORK?

The format will allow you to pick up this book and give a chapter a quick read in-between other tasks, or finish the entire book at a stretch. The chapters are ordered to make sense as a whole, but don't let that stop you from flipping through the book and starting with whoever catches your fancy. The mix of famous personas in this book ensures it has something for everybody—from the usual suspects Amitabh Bachchan, Steve Jobs and Thomas Edison to Albert Einstein, Nelson Mandela, Walt Disney, Vincent van Gogh, Serena Williams, Ratan Tata and even Lady Gaga. Each figure has been carefully chosen on the basis of their struggle and the impact they have had on the world. They had to fight against their own shortcomings, the system, society and sometimes nature itself to achieve their dreams. Their contributions are unparalleled—without them, we would not have the basic tenets of science; South Africa may not have had its first democratic elections; India's spirit of enterprise wouldn't have earned global respect; technological advancements in automobiles, computers, film and other arenas would be lagging; we would never have encountered some of our beloved childhood books and characters; sports would be missing some of its brightest gems; and art and music would feel incomplete.

Each chapter first introduces the individual in question and the effect their work has had on the world. The chapter then outlines their biography in chronological order for easier grasping, leading up to the point at which they found themselves at a crossroads. This is the bit that is of most significance to us. These legends faced hardships at several points, but it is this crossroads that determined the rest of their lives. Did they take Path 1 or Path 2, and what would we have done if we were in their shoes? The depiction of these paths is followed by the Lasting Lesson section; this is the moral of the story—how it applied in their lives and how we can absorb it in our own. Examples of situations in which we can implement these learnings are also mentioned, which makes them more relatable to our everyday lives. Finally, at the end of each chapter, there are a few fascinating facts on the person as an add-on of something you may not have known before.

This book aims to humanize those who may have been lost behind the myths and brands (and sometimes controversies) that shrouded their lives. No one was born a glorious ray of light. Each and every person in this book rose to the top through sheer hard work and determination. Their stories are inspiring because most of us are born in circumstances that don't always complement our aspirations. However, these celebrities are not meant to be placed on a pedestal to be worshipped, but to be viewed as human beings who've accomplished wonderful feats and can teach us from their experiences.

While learning about these individuals, I discovered lessons that I now apply in my daily life. That is why all the lessons are for 'us' to learn, and this book at no point diminishes the reader's intelligence or preaches to them from a higher moral stance. Biographies can be dull, especially for younger readers, and I wished to write this book in a way to make it as exciting and entertaining as reading a fictional story. There is no intended readership—the book is appropriate for all ages. I hope it is as enjoyable for you to read as it was for me to research and write, and that you will be inspired from these fantastic failures just as I was.

STRUGGLES ARE INEVITABLE

Amitabh Bachchan (b. 1942)

Bollywood actor

Success is very momentary... If there is no struggle in life, there is no life.

Amitabh Bachchan

What makes a superstar? A glorious long-lasting career, making game-changing moves? Or, perhaps, being worshipped as a god in temples? Without a doubt, all three are true in the case of the Shahenshah of Bollywood, the Star of the Millennium, the One-Man Industry: Amitabh Bachchan. In his remarkable career, he has starred in over 200 films, winning top-notch accolades such as the Dadasaheb Phalke Award, Padma Shri, Padma Bhushan and Padma Vibhushan, as well as numerous national film awards and lifetime achievement awards. His reputation has traversed the Indian border and spread worldwide: the French government conferred on him the title of Officer of the Legion of Honour, he was the first living Asian to have his wax model displayed at London's Madame Tussauds and he was voted the greatest star of stage or screen in a 1999 BBC online poll. Apart from acting in seminal films such as *Sholay, Deewar, Zanjeer* and *Black*, he has also produced films, sung playback and hosted the iconic *Kaun Banega Crorepati* that forced everyone home in time to tune in at nine on weeknights. Due to his philanthropic interests, he was also chosen by UNICEF as its Goodwill Ambassador in 2005.

With such illustrious achievements, one cannot be faulted for focusing only on Bachchan's golden years. From facing rejection to playing the leading man, from having numerous flops to experiencing a heady comeback, Bachchan has seen it all in a career spanning five decades. While he has shown great resilience, his life story—mirroring a roller coaster ride—is a humble reminder to us all that good fortune is no one's lifelong friend, even if you're a Jai or Veeru!

THE MAN WHO WOULD BE SHAHENSHAH

Amitabh Bachchan was born on 11 October 1942 in the city of Prayagraj (formerly known as Allahabad) in Uttar Pradesh. He is the firstborn of two sons of the acclaimed poet Harivansh Rai Bachchan and Teji Bachchan. His mother came from an affluent Sikh household in what is now known as Faisalabad in Pakistan, while his father hailed from a lower-middle-class Hindu family. The couple was an ardent supporter of the freedom struggle, and it is said that Teji ran to join a parade of the Quit India Movement when she was close to nine months pregnant with Bachchan and had to be pulled back by concerned friends and family. A friend had joked that if she had a son, she should name him Inquilab in honour of the slogan *Inquilab Zindabad*, meaning 'Long Live the Revolution.'

'Bachchan' was the nom de plume of the poet. When

asked for his son's full name at school admissions, Harivansh Rai used 'Amitabh Bachchan' for the first time as he was against caste discrimination and wished to avoid having his caste identified through the given last name. Bachchan studied briefly in Prayagraj before transitioning to the Sherwood College boarding school in Nainital. Excelling on the stage from a young age, Bachchan was awarded the Kendal Cup at Sherwood. He was the favourite candidate for the second year as well, but unfortunately he caught measles soon before his performance. His father, usually a strict disciplinarian, sat with the young Bachchan through the night of the play to distract his son from the applause and cheers drifting from the auditorium into the sick room. After school, he attended Kirori Mal College, University of Delhi, where he was also active in theatre. Upon graduating, he tried to venture into radio, which would seem like the perfect medium for his baritone. Shockingly, he was rejected as both a Hindi and English announcer by All India Radio (AIR) because his voice was deemed 'unsuitable'. Dejected and desperate for a job, he moved to Kolkata to work as a business executive, earning ₹500 a month, most of which went towards renting the room he shared with eight others. Throughout this period, he remained active in the theatre scene. In 1966, Bachchan applied to the Filmfare–Madhuri Talent Contest, believing it to be a legitimate entry point into Bollywood. Alas, he didn't even clear the preliminaries!

A restless Bachchan then decided to try his luck in the city where dreams were known to turn into reality—Mumbai. Though Bachchan grew up in a serious, literary atmosphere— besides being a Hindi poet and university lecturer, his father was also among the first Indians to complete a PhD in English literature from the University of Cambridge—he never felt any pressure from his parents to deviate from his chosen career path. In return, he didn't wish to lay any financial stress on them, so he preferred spending a few nights on a bench in Marine Drive than ask them for money. He later moved in with friends, created a portfolio and met with various industry bigwigs, who turned him away at the door after seeing his lanky 6'2" form. In the meantime, he made do by recording radio jingles. He had almost lost all hope when his brother heard of a casting call for fresh faces for *Saat Hindustani*, and Bachchan nabbed the role of one of the seven. The debut performance earned him a National Award for Best Newcomer in 1969. He was then offered *Anand* but not as the lead. He was to appear in a supporting role alongside the most in-demand actor of the day, Rajesh Khanna. Yet, Bachchan managed to shine in his smaller part. He was grateful for any sort of acting work that came his way, so he made short appearances in films such as *Reshma Aur Shera*. During this time, he met the actor Jaya Bhaduri, whom he would marry in 1973 and have two children with, Shweta and Abhishek. His first leading role came in the shape of *Bombay to Goa*, but it took many, many flops before he donned the hat of his first 'Vijay' character in the 1973 groundbreaking film, *Zanjeer*. This led to a slew of action roles in which his character fought against injustices of the system as the 'angry young man', reflecting the frustrations of the country around the time of the Emergency.

The seventies saw Bachchan rise to his peak with films such as *Deewar*, *Sholay*, *Amar Akbar Anthony* and *Don*. However, this period was also witness to rumours of Bachchan's involvement in the 1975 press censorship that accompanied the Emergency. His relationship with the media became strained, which resulted in a 15-year ban, beginning as a protest from the media. They printed a comma instead of his name in cast lists and denied photographing him at events, but it turned into a snub on Bachchan's part as he refused all interaction with the press.

In the next decade, Bachchan's luck took a turn for the worse on both personal and professional fronts. He was grievously injured in a fight sequence on the sets of *Coolie* in 1982. Nobody realized for the first 72 hours how severe his wound was, and when the surgeries were finally performed, he didn't wake from his coma. He was declared clinically dead for a few minutes, until a doctor made a Hail Mary pass and injected him with massive amounts of cortisone that revived him. He woke up to find that the entire country had united in praying for his health. As a mannat, or a vow, one man even ran backwards from Baroda to Mumbai to meet Bachchan. He took a break from acting in 1984 and made a brief stint in politics as a Member of Parliament upon the request of family friend Rajiv Gandhi after the assassination of then-Prime Minister Indira Gandhi. The actor gradually realized he had entered the new arena for emotional reasons and wasn't suited for the job. He resigned three years later. This coincided with a new trouble for the Bachchan clan—their entanglement in the Bofors scandal. The political controversy relating to a weapons contract between India and Sweden accused Bachchan and his brother Ajitabh, among several others, for accepting kickbacks from the Swedish company as they were close friends of the ruling Gandhis. Bachchan and his family began to be treated as traitors by a nation that had just a few years earlier prayed for his well-being. He fought the case in London courts, and his name was cleared after almost 25 years.

The nineties witnessed their own burdens. Bachchan took a brief hiatus from acting and set up Amitabh Bachchan Corporation Limited (ABCL) in an innovative effort to corporatize the Indian entertainment industry. However, as he was a novice at business who received ill-informed advice, his company faced a financial crisis and ended up owing its creditors close to ₹90 crore. He ultimately paid off the company's debts himself, thus losing all his assets in addition to having his public image destroyed, only to realize that taking a break from acting had been the wrong move. Newer faces had taken charge of the industry, and he was left with no offers that could ever match the prestige of his earlier work. After this long trek across high peaks and low valleys, Bachchan found himself at a crossroads:

Path 1

By no measure had Bachchan's journey been easy. It didn't matter how many magazine covers he graced, how many awards he won, fortune did not always favour him. His achievements couldn't stave off his losses, both material and emotional ones. Those who had been so keen to associate themselves with his name rebuffed him whenever his luck ran out. What would it take to exclusively climb higher heights? Where was his happy ending? He should give up already—there was no point in fighting any longer.

Path 2

Life isn't about climbing one particular mountain. Rather, it is about exploring an expanse—and to reach the next hill,

Bachchan had to trudge through the valley in between. It was like what his father had told him when Bachchan was bedridden with measles at Sherwood: *Jab tak jeevan hai, tab tak sangharsh hai,* meaning so long as there is life, there will be struggle. He had fought against all hardships, and as always, he would find a way out of the mist to catch sight of the next peak.

Due to stress, Bachchan was having trouble sleeping, so he arose at four in the morning one day. He acknowledged that he had limited control over how events turned out, but he knew that there was one thing he was good at—acting. He walked over to his neighbour Yash Chopra's house and implored for a role. Bachchan was offered a spot in *Mohabbatein,* which became a box-office hit. He didn't have the leading part—it wasn't even the second-biggest role—but it was something. Around the same time, he was approached to host a new TV show based on the popular British and American game show, *Who Wants to Be a Millionaire.* Despite his own reservations, along with those of his family and friends, about downgrading from the silver screen to the small screen, he accepted the offer. If truth be told, he needed paid work after all the financial losses he had incurred. Who would have guessed what a cultural phenomenon *Kaun Banega Crorepati* would become? All eyes in the country locked on Bachchan and his heart-warming interactions with regular folk. Terminology from the show entered everyday lingo as well: *'Lock kiya jaaye?'* became a household phrase meaning 'Is your decision final?', used before confirming a choice.

Bachchan realized that he would be relegated to supporting roles in films due to his advancing age, but he welcomed the change. He felt that character roles would allow him room to experiment in a way that he never could as an action or romantic lead. In the new millennium, he has delivered a rich variety of performances in hits such as *Kabhi Khushi Kabhie Gham...*, *Lakshya*, *Black*, *Sarkar*, *Paa* and *Piku*. While he is regarded as one of the best actors to ever emerge from Bollywood, he maintains an almost pessimistic attitude (though some may call it realistic) that things could go awry any day, and thus continues to work in his late seventies to retain financial independence.

LASTING LESSON

The first thing we are read to as children are fairy tales, in which the protagonist defeats the dragon, or the prince and princess wed and live happily ever after. Most films convey the same message too. However, in reality, our lives don't come to a standstill once we land our dream job or marry 'the one'. We're not shown what happens after the couple drives off into the sunset and we reach *The End*, but there *is* something that follows. Time, staying true to its nature, keeps ticking and every moment brings along a new challenge. Some we prevail at, others we don't. If we interpret those happy endings literally, we'll set up unrealistic expectations. Yet no achievement, no milestone can ensure unending bliss. Our joy is dependent upon infinite variables—health, positive relationships, career success, financial security— and not only ours, but also of our loved ones. Anything *can* go wrong and *will* go wrong one day. But, difficulties and mistakes mould and toughen us too so that we are better equipped the next time we fall.

As sad as it may sound, life is messy, life is gruelling, life is ridden with obstacles. Our aim isn't to climb Mount Everest and sit atop it for the rest of time. Our aim is to traverse through the Himalayas, and then who knows, perhaps there will be time to touch the Alps, Rocky Mountains and Andes as well. We will always come across plains and valleys, and it is good that we do. Because without them, how would we appreciate the view from the mountaintop? On our journey to get to not just that one scenic view but multiple ones, we have to remind ourselves that:

STRUGGLES ARE INEVITABLE.

Amitabh's Artistry

Honest and critical of his own work, Bachchan finds flaws in performances that even critics call perfect. In a scene in *Black*, he fishes out glasses from his shirt pocket to read a letter. Today, he is unable to watch a simple sequence like that without cringing because he believes he made an egregious error. His character suffers from Alzheimer's, which impacts a person's memory, so Bachchan believes he should have spent a few seconds patting all his pockets to look for the spectacles as his character wouldn't have been able to immediately recall where he had last kept them.

ADAPT, OR BECOME IRRELEVANT

Steve Jobs (1955–2011)

Co-founder of Apple Inc.

Death is very likely the single best invention of life. It's life's change agent—it clears out the old to make way for the new.

Steve Jobs

T he epithet 'visionary' is perhaps thrown around too freely, but it fits Steve Jobs—the man who led the personal computer revolution. By co-founding Apple, the first lifestyle brand in the realm of technology, he gave us products we didn't even know we wanted. He also made a mark in the telephone, music and entertainment industries. Besides having been the CEO and Chairman of Apple, he established another computer company, NeXT, and acquired Pixar, which The Walt Disney Company bought in 2006, making Jobs the largest individual shareholder of Disney. Though not the most skilled engineer, Jobs was one of those rare industrialists who gained the status of a rock star with a horde of loyal fans. This was all due to the tech he envisioned, his aesthetic sensibilities and the way he marketed himself and Apple. In fact, before his death in 2011, his net worth was $7 billion and Apple became the world's most valuable brand.

For his innovations, Jobs received several accolades, including the National Medal of Technology and Innovation as well as being conferred the titles of the Most Powerful Person in Business by *Fortune* and Entrepreneur of the Decade by *Inc.*

It almost makes sense that someone with such glorious achievements faced a fall, much like a Greek hero. The way in which Steve Jobs rose from his failures gave birth to his incredible fan-following and hero worship. He introduced principles of science and technology in the way he conducted business, and this ultimately made all the difference.

BEFORE THE VISIONARY

Steven Paul Jobs was born in California in the United States on 24 February 1955 to unwed college students, Joanne Schieble and Abdulfattah 'John' Jandali. Schieble gave the baby up for adoption to bookkeeper Clara and machinist and repo man Paul Jobs on the condition that the child must be allowed to attend college. The couple also adopted a girl later. Jobs grew up knowing that he wasn't his parents' biological child, and while he had a happy childhood in a small suburban house in Santa Clara Valley (soon to become Silicon Valley), he always felt like a rebel, a misfit, thinking the normal rules didn't apply to him.

Jobs was a bright child. His school wanted him to skip two grades, though his parents decided to have him skip one. He enjoyed watching his father build things and spend time on ensuring that the look and feel of the objects matched his particular standards (sound familiar?). Jobs gradually became interested in electronics and at age 12, he dialled Bill Hewlett of Hewlett-Packard to ask for any parts that he could spare so that Jobs could build a frequency counter. Not only did Hewlett laugh and agree, he gave Jobs a summer job at the company. Around this time, he met the tech whiz kid, Steve Wozniak, and despite their age difference—Wozniak was five years older—the two bonded over their shared love of electronics. Yet, Jobs never fit the clean-cut stereotype of the 'computer geek'. While he was fond of gadgets, he also enjoyed art and literature and became increasingly interested in the counterculture of the sixties. At 17, he joined the expensive Reed College, only to drop out six months later as he felt it wasn't worth spending all of his parents' savings. He had no clue about what he wanted to achieve in life and didn't see how college could help him figure that out. He wasn't against education or learning new skills; it was the rigidity of degrees and curriculum that he disliked. For the next year-and-a-half, he sat in on classes of his own choice and even took a course on calligraphy, where he learnt to appreciate the beauty of written text although it had no practical use in his life at the time.

In the early seventies, Jobs began working as a technician in the night shift at the videogame maker, Atari. He saved up to travel to India in search of spiritual enlightenment and returned a few months later with a shifted perspective and an urge to explore other spiritual schools of thought, such as Buddhism. He didn't perceive spirituality as being discordant with the material nature of technology. Wozniak and Jobs began fiddling with gadgets and built a 'blue box', which enabled them to make free phone calls around the world. They even tried prank-calling the Pope; alas, they couldn't directly speak with him. In 1976, Wozniak designed a personal computer and showed it to Jobs, who was amazed by it. While Wozniak found pleasure in building things, Jobs saw their sales potential. He suggested they sell it, though Wozniak wasn't convinced they'd be able to make any profit. But Jobs was happy with the mere prospect of creating a company, which they did in his family's garage, and named it Apple Computer. Many versions abound regarding the significance of the name, but Jobs stated once that he named it so because, as an erstwhile fruitarian, he liked apples and he wanted to appear before Atari in the phone book. The computer, Apple I, wasn't the kind we picture now. It was basically the brain of the computer that was supposed to be hooked up to a screen and keyboard by the customer, so they had to have some technical knowledge. When it came to the Apple II, Wozniak wished to introduce colour graphics. Jobs wanted Apple II to be an assembled product so that they could tap into the customer base that longed to mess around with programming, but didn't have the necessary know-how to put together a computer. With higher goals, Apple required more funding. They reached out to Mike Markkula, who invested as an equal partner in the company. Apple II, one of the first successful microcomputers, was released in 1977 to a great reception, making Jobs a millionaire.

On 12 December 1980, Apple went public and became worth nearly $2 billion by the end of the day. Such staggering success transformed the shape of the company. It obviously became larger—a huge change from the time when both Steves tinkered in the Jobses' garage—but with that, politics seeped in. Wozniak believed that while Jobs wanted to rise in the world as a businessman, he tied that in with his philosophy of delivering well-made products. However, after going public, the company's goal changed from that to increasing value for shareholders. Twenty-five-year-old Jobs began to be taken less and less seriously as industry veterans flooded in and formed the board of directors. External pressure from rival IBM also increased. In response, Jobs lured a seasoned chief executive in 1983 to steer the company through the storm— John Sculley, CEO of Pepsi—in a pitch that has now become the stuff of legend ('Do you want to sell sugar water for the rest of your life? Or, do you want to come with me and change the world?' *Who wouldn't say yes?*). His help was especially needed because Apple II was keeping the company afloat as new Apple products failed.

Jobs had visited XEROX's Palo Alto Research Center in 1979 and had been amazed at the technical innovations he'd seen, including the mouse and a graphical user interface that used icons, folders and windows. These were revolutionary technologies at the time. He sought permission to incorporate and improve the two in Apple's Macintosh computer, named after a variety of apple. He also called upon his calligraphy lessons at Reed College to help create beautiful typefaces for the computer. Apple II was revealed in 1984 by Jobs himself in a presentation that later became his signature style for annual new releases, and the launch was accompanied by a Super Bowl commercial that gained cult status. The Macintosh was the first real home computer for personal use, but while it was originally supposed to be priced at $1,000, it was released at $2,500—much too expensive for the market. When the sales numbers trickled in, they were less than half of what Apple had expected. This added to the tensions between one-time friends Jobs and Sculley, who had been butting heads regarding the direction Apple should take. Eventually, Jobs was asked to step down from heading the

Macintosh division due to claims of mismanagement. Still operating as if he ran a start-up in his hippy days and not a public company worth billions, Jobs decided upon a revolt to oust Sculley. When Sculley learnt of the coup, he confronted Jobs and used his years of experience battling office politics to turn the board in his favour, a decision that was later backed by Jobs's old friend, Mike Markkula. It was made clear to Jobs that although he wasn't technically fired, he was being made a figurehead who had no powers in operational matters. It ended with Jobs resigning from Apple, the company he had co-founded when he was 21, and running into his crossroads:

Path 1

Jobs may have lost his company, but he wasn't a poor man by any stretch of imagination. He didn't need to keep slogging if he wasn't wanted around. What did he have to prove to anyone anyway? He could sell his Apple shares and move to the Caribbean in an early retirement. Buy a gorgeous mansion on the beach and nap on lounge chairs under the bright sun. His new wife would sit by him while their children played in the sand. They would have a golden retriever, jumping into the clear blue waters and fetching a ball that their children threw. Many could only dream of such a life.

Path 2

The alternative seemed like a tranquil picture, but there was one problem: just as a career is not a substitute for the affections of our loved ones, this image of familial perfection couldn't fill the void that had been created by Jobs's original love, Apple. Money wasn't his priority, though it granted him the resources he needed to do what he really enjoyed—

work, experiment and innovate. Apple may have been stolen from him, but what was stopping him from taking all the learning—from his successes and failures—and applying it to his new, changed circumstances?

Steve Jobs focused on what would come next in his life, and aptly started a venture called NeXT. He had not forgotten Apple or the betrayal he believed he had faced and unfortunately didn't make up with Sculley ever again. This hurt further intensified the fire in his belly, making it roar for greater success and validation. He once again surrounded himself with what he called 'A' people—the best of the best— to create what he thought would be the next big thing in the educational technology market. He also invested in (and later fully controlled) the animation studio Pixar, owned by George Lucas of *Star Wars* fame. In 1995, Pixar produced *Toy Story*—the first computer-animated feature film that sparked the creation of one of the most profitable film genres today.

However, NeXT did not perform as well as Jobs expected, but what it did manage to do was pave the way for his return to Apple—an Apple that had rid itself of Sculley a few years earlier. Apple bought NeXT in 1996 and convinced Jobs to take the helm as the new CEO of the company, which was a few months away from declaring bankruptcy. In an unprecedented move to save Apple, Jobs partnered with Microsoft, the organization he had been warring against. In 1998, he launched the first iMac, the iconic candy-coloured personal computer whose software was powered by NeXT technology. It was soon followed by the first iPod in 2001 and the iTunes store, which changed the music industry forever. Jobs continued his streak of innovation and went on to release the iPhone and the iPad in 2007 and 2010, respectively. Unfortunately, his life was cut short. After battling pancreatic cancer for nearly a decade, Jobs passed away on 5 October 2011 at the age of 56, leaving behind his wife Laurene Powell and four children.

LASTING LESSON

While Jobs displayed the attributes of hard work and tenacity, the one that particularly stood out was his power to *adapt*. He learnt to adapt to Apple's growing size during his second stint with the company and tackled the obstacles that were hurled at him at difficult times. Above all else, the secret to his success was constant innovation to adapt to the changing times. The amount of technological advancement that took place in his lifespan is incredulous. When Apple first started, the World Wide Web did not exist, and now our wireless phones—which can fit into the pockets of skinny jeans— seem like bricks if they're not connected to the Internet as a hyphenated 'e' has been inserted in front of everything— mail, commerce, banking, books, and so on.

This skill of adaptability isn't specific to the domain of work. It's also applicable in our personal lives, but more than that, it's showcased in nature. What is evolution but living beings adapting to their changing environments to become better, more efficient forms of life? And what is natural selection but the onward march of beings that excel at adaptation? We must embody these spirits, whether it's by keeping in touch with new technologies and processes, joining online courses to stay updated or simply doing our own research. If there is one thing that life can promise us, it is that it will never remain the same. We should face, no, welcome these changes—be it in our relationships, our personal circumstances or our work life—and thrive. And so, the negative saying 'Kill, or be killed', a business tactic that is ruthless in its attitude to fellow individuals, can be amended to keep it focused on what *we* can do for ourselves:

ADAPT, OR BECOME IRRELEVANT.

Steve and Sean

In 1984, Steve Jobs was invited along by a journalist friend to attend the ninth birthday party of Sean Lennon, the son of John Lennon of *The Beatles*. Jobs brought a present for the young boy, a Macintosh computer. Jobs placed it on the floor, put on MacPaint and showed Sean how to use the mouse, and Sean quickly began drawing. Among the merrymakers was the acclaimed artist, Andy Warhol. He sat between Steve and Sean and lifted the mouse off the ground to move it. Jobs guided him on how to use it properly (remember, this was the first mass computer to have a mouse). Soon, a big smile spread across Warhol's face as he turned to the other guests and announced that he had drawn a circle.

WE ARE NOT OUR CIRCUMSTANCES

Oprah Winfrey (b. 1954)

TV personality

Although there may be tragedy in your life, there's always a possibility to triumph. It doesn't matter who you are, where you come from. And the ability to triumph begins with you, always. Always.

Oprah Winfrey

Not many people in this world can claim to be recognized by solely their first name, but one such figure is the 'Queen of All Media', Oprah. She rose to international fame through her talk show, *The Oprah Winfrey Show*, which ran for 25 years until its final season in 2011. She's often counted among the world's most dedicated philanthropists, and even founded a school for girls in South Africa. While she is best known for her show in which she interviewed over 35,000 people, she has diversified her portfolio to encompass other forms of media, such as film, publishing, radio and the Internet. Proving her acting chops in *The Color Purple* and *Beloved*, she went on to showcase her entrepreneurial skills by launching the Oprah Winfrey Network, or OWN. She should also be known as the 'Queen of Firsts'—she was the first woman to own and produce her own talk show as well as the first African-American woman to enter *Forbes* magazine's list of World's Richest People and be awarded the Cecil B. DeMille Award. It's really no surprise that she's worth over $2.5 billion today.

Sixty-six-years old but showing no signs of slowing down, Oprah is considered one of the most influential people on earth. Whatever she vouches for turns to gold. With such powers must come a story comparable to an epic, replete with its tragedies and surprise twists. Almost everyone she knew bet against her, but they made the mistake of not taking into account her belief that she held the keys to her destiny.

THE WOMAN BEFORE THE MONONYM

Prior to becoming *the* Oprah, she was Oprah Gail Winfrey (though her birth certificate said 'Orpah'), a baby born to an unmarried teenage girl in rural Mississippi, United States, on 29 January 1954. Her father Vernon Winfrey was enlisted in the army and away at a base when he received news of the birth. Shortly after Oprah was born, her mother Vernita Lee went away as part of the Great Migration, which was the movement of millions of African Americans from the southern states to other parts of the country. Like the countless Black youngsters handed over to their relatives to be raised at that time, baby Oprah was left with her grandmother Hattie Mae. The grandmother wasn't well off, living in a house without running water or electricity. She had been educated till the third grade, and both she and Lee worked as domestic help, so that was the future they envisioned for Oprah as well.

Although Hattie Mae ran a strict household, even whipping her granddaughter on many occasions, Oprah claims the older woman saved her life by teaching her significant skills: to read at an unusually early age and speak eloquently. By age three, Oprah was reciting speeches at church. The nuns complimented the young girl, calling her gifted. So, it became custom for Oprah to recite Bible verses and poetry for anyone who visited their home.

At age six, Oprah was sent to Milwaukee to live with her mother who had birthed another daughter by then. Oprah knew then that she would never again see the only family she had known, her grandmother. The mother and two daughters lived in a small one-room apartment. Lee worked long hours, so Oprah was often left in the care of male relatives. A vulnerable child, she was raped at age nine by a cousin and molested between the ages of 10 and 14 by relatives and a family friend. These horrific instances became so frequent in the young girl's life that she thought them the norm. Shamed and threatened by the perpetrators, she hid these harrowing experiences all the way into her late twenties. But trauma cannot be suppressed for long; it impacted her life and caused behavioural problems. She began acting out and once even ran away from home. Oprah became pregnant at 14, but hid the fact for seven months because she feared for her life. Her mother wanted her gone and took Oprah to a detention home. Seeing other disturbed youth around her, Oprah realized that she would be officially labelled a 'bad girl' by society although she didn't feel like one inside. In a serendipitous turn of events, Lee was informed that the home was full and there wouldn't be a place for the young girl for two weeks. Oprah thus got another chance to live with family, and she was sent away to live with her father and stepmother in Nashville, Tennessee.

Vernon Winfrey ran a tight ship. He set a curfew for his teenage daughter and told her to read a new book every week and submit a report on it to him. He also informed her that he would rather she died than bring 'shame' to the family. Without a sympathetic ear around, Oprah continued hiding the pregnancy. Lonely and afraid of how society would treat her as an unwed mother, she inflicted harm on herself and contemplated suicide. She eventually gave birth but the baby died in hospital, and she returned to school shortly after. Her father told her that through these devastating circumstances, she had been given a second chance at life. Oprah vowed to seize it. She began excelling at studies and extra-curricular activities, such as plays and speeches, and was elected head of the student council. This turnaround started a chain reaction that attracted her subsequent successes.

Sixteen-year-old Oprah was chosen to attend a White House conference, and a local radio station interviewed her about it. Her confidence and command over language created such an impression on the folks at the station that when they needed to nominate a teenager to enter the Miss Fire Prevention contest a year later, they recalled Oprah. She was the lone African-American contestant and assumed her chances at winning were nil. As a consequence, she felt freed from the pressures of the competition and was completely herself on stage. In the question–answer round, she was asked what career she would like to pursue. She responded with broadcast journalism, purely because she wanted to provide a unique answer and had watched the famous journalist Barbara Walters on TV earlier that day.

As fate would have it, just as the words escaped her mouth, something clicked—not only within her regarding her career choice, but at the competition too. Oprah won. Later, when she went to claim her prize from the radio station, they asked her whether she'd like to hear her voice on tape and thus had her read a copy. She blew everyone away and was offered a job on the spot, which she worked at after school every day.

Oprah joined Tennessee State University on full scholarship. At 19, she was approached by a reputed local TV news channel for the position of an on-air reporter. She turned it down initially, believing she wouldn't be able to manage full-time employment along with her studies, until one of her professors told her that people went to university *hoping* they would receive such a call one day. She took his advice to heart and became the youngest and first female news anchor for the channel in Nashville. She was an instant hit. Three years later, she moved to a higher-profile channel in Baltimore, Maryland. Throughout her time on TV, she modelled herself after Barbara Walters—the person she had compared herself to at the pageant.

However, Oprah wasn't like other journalists. When reporting on a house fire, she offered blankets to the victims and told parents who had lost their children that they didn't have to speak with her about the incident. She was too passionate, too empathetic—and the bosses noted it. She got told off for this humane trait, for caring too much about people rather than the scoop. Moreover, the management felt she didn't *look* the part of a newscaster—that her hair was too thick, her eyes too far apart, her nose too wide! In other words, they criticized her for her racial features. She was sent to a fancy New York City salon for a 'makeover'. More likely, they tried to *make her over* into someone she wasn't. Their attempt at a perm utterly failed and ruined her hair, making it all fall off. Not willing to keep her on anymore nor wanting to pay out her contract, the management hit upon what they thought was a creative solution—to demote her to a morning slot, making her chance upon her crossroads:

Path 1

Oh, Oprah knew she was close to being fired. She might be young, but she was no fool. She was aware of the whispers around her. She'd had a good ride the past couple of years, but who was she kidding? Good things didn't happen to her. Her shot at radio and fame on TV were freaks of fortune. Born into poverty, deprived of a mother's love, repeatedly sent away, physically and sexually abused, impregnated at a young age—that's who Oprah had been. Who was she to fight fate? She should find a sensible job like her relatives and be content with her lot in life.

Path 2

One clear distinction remained between the agonizing experiences of her childhood and this conundrum at work— *choice*. She did not choose to be born into hardship, she did not choose to repeatedly relocate in her childhood and her choice was stolen from her at every instance of abuse. As an adult now, she could take a stand and entirely own who she was. She had Oprah's face and heart, not that of any other newscaster. So, she would interact with guests on the morning talk show as she deemed fit and connect with other human beings. What's the worst that could happen that wasn't already on the verge of occurring?

Oprah's decision to shed the skin of an unbiased journalist, with which she had always felt a disconnect, and be her own person on *People Are Talking* is the exact reason that every viewer fell in love with her—her authenticity and openness. She honed her skills in the late 1970s and redefined the genre of talk shows. The spontaneous back-and-forth of actual human interaction where she was more concerned with listening to others than spewing eloquent phrases suited her. Her success on what was supposed to be a demotion led to her independent talk show in Chicago, one of the largest markets in the US. Oprah soon became a household name due to her obvious talent and mass appeal, and the show was eventually renamed from *AM Chicago* to *The Oprah Winfrey Show*. Other talk shows did prop up, but they were focused on orchestrating confrontations for cheap thrills. While the earlier episodes of Oprah's show were guilty of this practice too, she repurposed the format to make it more uplifting and spiritual. This cost her in the ratings initially, but her audience soon grew to admire her for it. It's also what she ascribes the longevity of her show to—from six million homes in the US in 1986, she ultimately reached the screens of over a hundred countries. That very same year, she met Stedman Graham, now her partner for over 30 years.

LASTING LESSON

Life isn't a smooth ride. Not one among us is born into ideal circumstances or faces zero obstacles. It is true that some encounter much tougher troubles than others, and allowances must be made to let them cope in the way they choose. We should try not to despair as there's always hope, a possibility to prevail. Metal is forged by hammer and anvil, but this external force does not change its elemental nature. While our experiences shape who we become, how much power we grant them depends wholly on us.

Many use the terms 'fate' and 'destiny' interchangeably, but they are not the same. We can be resigned to our fates and believe we have no control over what happens to us. Or, we could explore possibilities and work towards the potential of our destinies. Yes, life can be random and unfair, and we cannot exert our authority over every single aspect of the universe, but we do have choice. We make thousands of choices every day that many of us are fortunate to have full control over—what time to wake up, what to eat, whether to exercise, what kind of work to do, how to react to confrontations. We operate within the paradigm of our circumstances, but they can be moulded by the sheer force of our will too. Life isn't about living through the motions as a passive spectator. After all, we all get one shot at this, so we might as well be active participants and carve our own way. We must remember that our destiny is in our own hands, since:

WE ARE NOT OUR CIRCUMSTANCES.

Open-hearted Oprah

The trauma Oprah faced as a child is enough to permanently scar and change a person. She had every right to hold on to it. But, not only did she choose to stride forward, she also used her platform and influence to fight for justice for others who were at risk. In 1991, she testified before the US Senate Judiciary Committee and spoke of her childhood experiences with abuse. Her aim was to support the National Child Protection Act, which asked for the establishment of a national database of convicted child abusers. It was passed in 1993 and dubbed the 'Oprah Bill'.

HOW WE PLAY COUNTS MORE THAN WINNING

Lionel Messi (b. 1987)

Footballer

Obviously I don't like to lose or tie, but I'm looking at it in another way... There are many more important things than results.

Lionel Messi (translated)

The man with the golden foot also happens to be the highest-paid athlete with a net worth of a whopping $127 million. Argentinian footballer Lionel Messi is widely considered one of the best the sport has ever seen. He has almost every claim to fame a footballer can make, including the Ballon d'Or, European Golden Shoe, Olympic gold medal, UEFA Champions League title and FIFA World Youth Championship. Over the years, he has broken several records both in the history of his club, FC Barcelona, and on an international level. He isn't simply a goal-scoring machine; he's known for his creative plays and helping his teammates score, as well as his captainship of both FC Barcelona and the Argentina national team. It's no wonder that he's backed by big-time sponsors such as Adidas and Pepsi. Currently under construction in China, the world's largest theme park dedicated to football bears his name and hopes to see upwards of 40 million visitors every year. Off the pitch, Messi devotes his time to philanthropic activities as a UNICEF Goodwill Ambassador and through his foundation, Fundación Leo Messi, which provides vulnerable children access to education and healthcare.

It is no accident that Messi supports rising footballers in his home country and empathizes with at-risk youth. As a child, he was diagnosed with a health disorder that could have ended his football career before it even began. His determination to fight against the cards he had been dealt in life opened up new avenues and set the tone for how he would face obstacles later.

THE MAN IN THE #10 JERSEY

Lionel Andrés Messi was born on 24 June 1987 in Rosario, Argentina, to a family that adored football. His father Jorge was employed at a steel factory and his mother Celia in a magnet manufacturing workshop. Messi is the third of four children, with two elder brothers and one younger sister, and grew up watching his brothers and cousins play football on the neighbourhood streets. People familiar with the city of Rosario knew better than to drive their cars in the inner lanes filled with football-playing children. Indeed, the sport is a part of the city's culture. Messi himself began tossing the ball around when he was about three years old, spurred on by his supportive maternal grandmother, also named Celia. When he was five, she accompanied him to a game of a local club, Grandoli. The match was held up because a player was missing, so she asked the coach to let her grandson play instead. Although just a year younger, he was much smaller than the other kids, and the coach refused. Not one to back down, she reportedly entered a heated argument with the adamant coach, who declared there was no way he would change his mind. A few minutes later, little Leo walked to the field, thanks to his firebrand grandmother. The coach's bruised ego was soon forgotten as Messi scored twice.

Messi played for Grandoli for a while, later transferring to the iconic Argentine club, Newell's Old Boys. From the very beginning he captured everyone's attention with his innate talent. The football became a permanent accessory of his, and when he couldn't get his hands on one, his yearning feet kicked around plastic bottles and crumpled balls of paper. He was a natural at the sport despite his diminutive size. Always the smallest and frailest among his peers, his anxious parents took him to a doctor, who diagnosed 11-year-old Messi with a growth hormone deficiency. Without treatment, he was at risk of not growing any further and thus never attaining his dream of becoming a pro footballer. The treatment involved an injection that the pre-teen Messi himself administered every night alternatively in each leg. It was however a costly affair that his middle-class family couldn't afford on their own. They sought aid from local football clubs, but promises were broken as circumstances toughened due to the Argentinian economy not faring well. Luckily, the family heard from Spain's Barcelona Football Club; they had seen a video of Messi's spectacular talent and agreed to pay for his treatment with the condition that he moved to the city. Finding it too good an opportunity to pass up, the family agreed and left for Barcelona. The move was hard on his siblings though. Torn among his children, one day Messi's father sat the 13-year-old down and asked him if he would like to return to Argentina as well. Keeping his eyes set on his goal, Messi chose to stay, knowing fully well that he was in for a long difficult ride as his mother and siblings returned to Rosario while his father remained with him in Barcelona. Messi's dream was *so close*—playing for a club he had always admired while having the chance to treat his medical condition.

Having left behind the only life he had known—his country, school, friends and family—Messi was terribly homesick, and even today recalls this period as being the toughest in his life. Being a shy kid, he didn't interact much with other young players to the extent that on the first day in the locker room, his teammates believed him to be mute. It didn't help matters that he couldn't speak the local Catalan. But he didn't need words on the field. There, his skill and drive spoke for themselves. During a game at age 17, he took a jab to the face that fractured his cheekbone; days after the injury, he entered the field wearing a face mask that was deemed compulsory, but he took it off after a few minutes as it hampered his sight and scored twice before he was pulled out for his own safety. He continued his hormonal treatment—although some days he had to avoid playing as he needed rest after the injections—and his body grew as it should have on its own. He became stronger and taller, eventually reaching 5'7". He climbed ranks quickly over the years, playing for the Barcelona B team before he was offered his first senior contract on his eighteenth birthday with a buyout clause of €150 million. Within a few months, his wages were reportedly doubled as the entire world caught the Messi fever.

On 1 May 2005, Messi scored his first goal for the Barcelona First Team in a competitive match and went on to wow spectators and players alike with his agility and dribbling. He was a beast on the field—opposing teams were forced to have not one but two or three of their players surround him, yet he whizzed past them with thoughtful footwork and incredible speed. After scoring a goal, he would point both index fingers up to the heavens as a way of thanking god and remembering his grandmother whom he lost in 1998. It has since become his signature style.

At his adoptive home Barcelona, Messi collected one accolade after another, but something was amiss. While he played for his country Argentina—even bringing home the 2005 FIFA World Youth Championship and the 2008 Olympic gold medal—he could not replicate Barcelona's continued winning streak for it. This led to backlash from Argentinian fans and press after every loss, so much so that they questioned Messi's loyalty to his motherland. Despite being the country's top goal-scorer, he failed to claim an international title in either the World Cup or the South American championship, Copa América. He reached an especially low point in the 2016 Copa América Centenario, in which he missed a penalty shootout and lost to Chile in the finals. The expectations that not just the Argentinian citizens had of him but he had of himself were dashed in his fourth finals' loss. It overwhelmed him, bringing him to a crossroads:

Path 1

Messi had been trying his best, but something wasn't clicking for him in Argentina. And the nation held him responsible. Why did he play for a team that never seemed to win, especially when the country so readily denounced him? It was like they forgot that football was a team sport and the manager and coach also played significant roles. Messi won the best player awards as an Argentine team member even when the team lost, so obviously it wasn't as if he didn't perform. He was heralded as a hero in Spain, playing for one of the top football clubs on earth. It was right to retire from international football. Why should he continue reducing his star power with every failure Argentina faced?

Path 2

Stardom wasn't the reason Messi got into the sport in the first place though. Sure, fame and money were great, but through sickness, loneliness and injuries, he pursued the game because he lived and breathed football. It was that drive, that determination that had pushed him to claim European championships. It's what converted Lionel into *Messi*. And it would now be out of character for him to give up on an aspiration he'd held since he was a child—to win a title for his nation.

Although Messi announced his retirement from international football after the 2016 Copa América debacle, he reversed his decision a month later, much to the country's collective relief. He accomplished one of his famed hat-tricks in the 2018 World Cup to help Argentina qualify for the tournament in a 3–1 game against Ecuador. While Argentina didn't win the cup, Messi's performance helped the country save face in the qualifiers. He still hopes to nab an international title for his birth country, or at least try his best as many times as he can, while he continues dazzling at Barcelona. He's the top scorer in the Spanish league, La Liga, with over a 100 more goals than any other player. During his time on the team, Barcelona has accomplished historic two trebles by winning La Liga, Copa del Rey and the Union of European Football Associations (UEFA) Champions League all in one season. In May 2019, he scored his 600th goal on the exact day he made his first-ever goal for the club 14 years prior. He married his childhood sweetheart Antonela Roccuzzo in 2017 and has three children with her.

LASTING LESSON

We've all heard the cliché, 'It's not about the destination, but the journey.' While achieving our aims is important (otherwise, why would we bother trying?), *how* we achieve them is just as much, if not more, crucial. Whether it's about ethics, morality or staying true to who we are, the way we conduct ourselves matters. If our lives were mapped out as one chronological story about attaining a particular goal, each decision we made would be a point that revealed our characters, showed the kind of mark we left on the world.

Most of us worry about our reputations, but even if some don't, we all care about how we perceive our own selves. There are certain values we aspire to, certain actions we hold ourselves accountable for. And at the end of the day, we all have to live with ourselves. It would probably be easier to live as Messi—someone who hasn't yet achieved an aim but continues to strive for it after disheartening losses because that's who he is as a person—than compromising ourselves by behaving in a way that might go against our nature. Take the example of a competition or an exam: we could cheat our way through it, but doing so would mar the win for us because *we* would always know that we didn't deserve it. Or, we could not bother giving it our all because we're afraid of losing. But then we may never find out what we're truly capable of.

There's a reason why everyone offers the consolation, 'At least you tried your best.' Yes, we're in competition with others but also with ourselves. Knowing that we gave our 100 per cent and being content with our actions make the failures easier to accept and help us understand how we can improve in the future. If ever the pressure of winning seems to push us into a corner we're not comfortable with, all we have to do is remind ourselves that:

HOW WE PLAY COUNTS MORE THAN WINNING.

Messi's Moxie

As a young footballer in Argentina, Messi once got locked in his bathroom during a tournament final. All members of the winning team were supposed to receive bicycles, so Messi and the other kids were keen on victory. Rather than miss the match, Messi broke the glass of the door to escape and reached in time for the second half. He scored a hat-trick and beat the other team 3–1, thus nabbing bikes for all his friends and himself.

SAY YES TO SMART RISKS

Richard Branson (b. 1950)

Co-founder of Virgin Group

Protecting the downside is critical. So, we'll make bold moves, but we'll also make sure we've got ways out if things go wrong.

Richard Branson

Entrepreneur, philanthropist and daredevil: these three words encapsulate Sir Richard Branson, the man who built one of the most exciting brands on earth, Virgin. With close to 69,000 employees in 35 countries working across various fields, the brand's annual revenue adds up to £16.6 billion. By being involved in the disparate spheres of music, mobile phones, banking, airlines, trains and space travel, Virgin has hardly obeyed any set business rule. With its non-profit foundation Virgin Unite, the organization has collaborated on projects such as The Elders (originally headed by Nelson Mandela), Carbon War Room and The Branson Centre for Entrepreneurship. Personally worth $4 billion, Branson has received several honours in appreciation of his work—he was presented with the United Nations Correspondents Association Citizen of the Year Award, counted among the *Time* 100 Most Influential People in the

World and even knighted for his services to entrepreneurship.

Famously known as 'Dr Yes' within the company for his tendency to meet every challenge head on, Branson's risk-taking hasn't always yielded positive results. However, this habit has taught him an important lesson on how to safeguard himself in business deals, and it's the advice he routinely offers to aspiring entrepreneurs as words to live by.

THE MAN, THE DAREDEVIL

Richard Charles Nicholas Branson was born on 18 July 1950 in London, United Kingdom, and grew up in a small village in Surrey. His father Edward was a barrister, following the family tradition of entering law. He married Eve, a flight attendant, and had three children with her—Branson and his two younger sisters.

Branson's mother played a significant role in shaping his personality. An adventurer herself, she wanted her children to be independent and at times used ways we would today consider extreme. When Branson was four, his mother chucked him out of the car for misbehaving and told him to walk the remaining few kilometres to their house. He reached home safely to find his mother waiting for him, worried. Branson was sent to a preparatory school and later attended the boarding school Stowe. Homesick in the early years, his misery further increased due to bad performance in academics. He suffers from dyslexia, a learning disorder, though it went undiagnosed at the time. Still, that didn't hinder the development of his entrepreneurial spirit at a young age, and he began his first venture at age 11 with best friend Nik Powell. They bred and sold budgies (a long-tailed parrot), but the birds multiplied too quickly and Branson's mother had to finally set them free. After that, Branson tried growing Christmas trees to sell during the holiday season; unfortunately, rabbits got to them.

In the 1960s, Branson empathized with the frustrations of his peers who wanted to interact with and exert their influence upon the tumultuous world around them. To provide them a national platform, 15-year-old Branson and a friend started their own magazine, *Student*. From this very first business, Branson displayed his daring nature. To meet the costs of creating the first issue, he needed to sell advertising space. He used the school phone box as his office and (unwittingly at first) the phone operators as his assistants: once, he lost a coin while dialling, so he called the operator who offered to ring the business he wanted to reach and informed them that Mr Branson was on the line for them. By repeating the lost-coin story with different operators, he realized that he could appear as a big-shot professional with his own assistant and moreover, make business calls for free. He quickly learnt tricks like enticing a company by telling them that their competitor had bought an entire page's worth of advertising, even if it wasn't always true. It eventually worked out for everyone as the big companies needed a way to reach out to the day's youth and no other magazine catered to that age group. Soon enough, his extracurricular activities came to the attention of school authorities. Summoned to the headmaster's office one day, Branson was given an ultimatum: either continue school and leave the magazine behind, or quit the school. He chose the latter since conventional teaching wasn't working for him due to his dyslexia. When his father found out, he gave Branson a talk about responsibilities and the importance of education. It ended with his father conceding that he hadn't known what he wanted in his early twenties, so if Branson was sure, he should give the magazine a shot. In case it failed, they could look at formal schooling again.

Running the magazine became Branson's education instead. Formally launched in 1968, *Student* gave youngsters across the country a chance to voice their opinions. One of the pertinent issues they tackled was the unjustness of the Vietnam War. When Branson required funds to meet the day-to-day functioning of the magazine, luck favoured him once more. His mother discovered a lost necklace and deposited it at the police station. It went unclaimed for months, so the police returned it to her. She sold it for £100, which she gave to her son. Alas, while the magazine had gained a circulation of 50,000, it didn't earn much profit. This led to the incorporation of another business idea into the magazine: a mail-order record company. Branson and his friends believed that they were attuned to the more popular, rock 'n' roll music of the time, and could offer it at a discount to the magazine readers. When it came to picking a name, a friend joked that since they were all virgins at doing business, why not embrace that identity? And that's how Virgin was born in 1970.

The business, in partnership with Branson's old friend Nik Powell, took off. It paid for the magazine and then some, enabling them to open the first Virgin Records shop on Oxford Street, London. The physical space was bought partly because of a 1971 postal strike that could've destroyed the company before it had hit its stride. One day, a musician handed a sample of his music to Branson, who thought it was terrific. He helped shop it around to several record labels, but none took it on. Branson couldn't believe their blindness to the album's potential, so he began his own production company in 1972 that went on to sign acts such as The Sex Pistols, The Rolling Stones and Janet Jackson. And that first musician, Mike Oldfield, hit the jackpot when the opening track from his album *Tubular Bells* became the theme song of the cult film, *The Exorcist*. The album's success made Branson, who was not yet 23, a millionaire.

Branson eventually shut down *Student* to focus full-time on the music business. In 1978, he was waiting at an airport in Puerto Rico to travel to the British Virgin Islands when his flight was cancelled as it didn't have enough passengers. Annoyed, he chartered a jet and divided the cost by the number of seats it held. On a borrowed blackboard he wrote: Virgin Airlines, one-way BVI $39. He thus managed to make the plane-hire a feasible exercise and when they landed, a passenger next to Branson told him that if he sharpened the service a bit, he could be in the airline business. As one does, the very next day Branson called Boeing and asked if they had any second-hand 747 planes to sell. They did. He told them he wished to start his own airline and would buy a plane on the condition that if the business didn't take off in a year, he could return the plane. Amused by this industry-outsider's call, they humoured him to see whether he could stand up to the big British airline of the time: British Airways, also known as BA.

And Branson did. He launched Virgin Atlantic in 1984 with one plane flying on one route but offering features that no other airline did. Virgin Atlantic was the first to have screens on the back of all seats and stand-up bars in upper-class cabins. Such amenities were accompanied by a marked difference in the quality of the service too. The number of planes the company owned gradually increased, though it was still a small airline compared to the major-league ones of the time. In 1990, BA launched a 'dirty tricks' campaign in which they hacked Virgin Atlantic's systems to access their customer data. BA would call up their competitor's passengers under false pretences and tell them that their flights had been cancelled and they should shift to BA instead. There were also reports of people rummaging through rubbish bins of Branson's other businesses in search of some ammunition against him. Such underhanded tricks adversely affected the fledgling Virgin Atlantic, which didn't have the resources to take on the behemoth, forcing Branson to his crossroads:

Path 1

Branson had finally done it. He had challenged fate and the status quo one too many times, and this was going to be his downfall. Why did he have to go shake things up? He had been doing just fine—no, *amazingly* even—with his record business, and he should have focused on growing it. Or, perhaps, finding other niche spaces that no one had thought of before. What made him think he could challenge an industry giant like BA when he didn't have their long history, market share or capital? He should shut down the airline—there was no use.

Path 2

Taking risks and making bold choices were part of Branson's MO. The stakes were higher here, but he knew he had a good thing going with the award-winning Virgin Atlantic. Furthermore, he had been in the right. He had all the evidence to fight too, but he needed financial backing to confront the monolith. There was one thing left to do: sell his record company and use that money to sue BA.

With a broken heart, Branson sold Virgin Records—the top independent record company of the world—to Thorn EMI for $1 billion in 1992. People reading the news splashed on every front page must have thought him excited on becoming a billionaire; yet, he was upset at losing the company he had built from the ground up. Albeit, he felt it was the best way to secure the jobs of the record company employees as well as the future of Virgin Atlantic. He took BA to court and won the largest libel case settlement in British history. As it was Christmastime, he distributed the money among Virgin Atlantic employees as 'BA Christmas bonus'. Since then, Branson's airline has become one of the primary players.

After setting up Virgin Atlantic, it has become the core of Branson's business persona to look at industries where better quality goods and services can be offered, and enter and disrupt those markets. Not all have met with great success, such as Virgin Cola, Virgin Brides and Virgin Cars. He has kept each company separate so that no one failure would bring the entire group down, and he hasn't declared bankruptcy yet. Indeed, he takes great care to protect the Virgin brand. He maintains a healthy work–life balance by spending quality time with his wife Joan Templeman, two children and their families, as well as mostly functioning from home, which happens to be an island that he bought in the 1970s. He has authored several books, and his *Screw It, Let's Do It* perhaps best epitomizes his philosophy on life.

LASTING LESSON

We can't make a splash in a puddle unless we jump. As kids, we're not bothered by the mess we make. When we grow older, we avoid this dicey 'childish' move in fear of dirtying our clothes and soaking our feet. But, what if one day we crossed a muddy patch while wearing rubber boots? Who among us wouldn't be tempted to hop into the puddle once more? Taking risks, venturing into unknown territories and meeting new challenges add flavour to our lives and keep things interesting. Yet, they need to be balanced by some precautions. Just as no one would be okay skydiving without knowing for certain that their parachute would work, whenever we attempt something bold and tricky, we have to ensure we've got safeguards in place to cushion us if we fail. This becomes especially critical if our livelihoods and our health and safety, or that of our loved ones, are at stake. If someone is keen on adopting a dog for the first time, they could try fostering a pet for a while to make sure they enjoy taking care of a canine and are prepared for it. While experimenting with a tough new cooking recipe, we could check beforehand to ensure restaurants can deliver food in case the meal goes awry! Analysing what exactly is at stake with each new bet we make can help us decide whether it's worth it, but we shouldn't let fear incapacitate us either. Remember, no new ground could ever be broken without gutsy movers and shakers, so:

SAY YES TO SMART RISKS.

Richard Roused

The school headmaster told Branson when he was leaving school that he would either become a millionaire or go to jail, and defying all odds, he did both. During the early days of Virgin Record shops, a customer from Belgium placed a bulk order. Branson took it by road, only to run into some trouble with papers in France and was forced to turn back. Upon returning, he realized that since the albums had been marked for export and thus exempted from heavy tax levied on music meant for the domestic market, the records could now be sold in the UK for cheaper and at higher profit. However, he was unaware that this scheme was being carried out in a much grander scale by bigger corporations, so the authorities already had their eyes peeled out for it. As a result, Branson was arrested for tax evasion and put in jail for a night. His mother had to pledge their family home as bail, and Branson learnt that he had to do everything in his power to avoid risking jailtime again. As he had been treating the shop lightly, he today thanks this incident for spurring him on to expand the business by opening several other Virgin Record shops in order to pay the fine for his offence.

At the time of this book being sent to print, there has been more recent news of Virgin Atlantic being in troubled waters.

FIND JOY IN WORK

Vincent van Gogh (1853–1890)

Painter

*So then my brush goes between my fingers as if it were
a bow on the violin and absolutely for my pleasure.*

Vincent van Gogh

Considered one of the legends of the Western art world, Vincent Van Gogh created close to 900 paintings in his short life of 37 years. Even a century after his tragic death, the Dutch post-Impressionist painter continues to inspire artists and art-lovers alike. Seminal pieces such as *The Starry Night, Sunflowers, Café Terrace at Night, Portrait of Dr. Gachet* and his self-portraits capture the bold colours and emotionally rendered subjects that he's renowned for. His artworks are some of the most sought after and costliest to own. In fact, *Portrait of Dr. Gachet* was sold at an auction in 1990 for $82.5 million, the largest sum paid at the time for a painting. There is a dedicated museum for the artist in his home country, the Netherlands, and his work is on display in prime art galleries across the globe, such as Museum of Modern Art in New York City, The National Gallery in London, Musée d'Orsay in Paris, and so on.

Unfortunately, van Gogh has become synonymous with

the idea of the 'tortured artist' and 'mad genius'. In these caricatures, we lose the man behind the myth: a man who went through several career changes to find the one that fit.

THE MAN, THE MYTH, THE ARTIST

The oldest child of pastor Theodorus van Gogh and his strict religious wife Anna Carbentus, Vincent van Gogh was born on 30 March 1853 in Zundert in southern Netherlands. He had five siblings—two brothers and three sisters—but in later life, retained contact with two, his brother Theo and sister Wil. Most of what the world knows today about van Gogh is through the letters that he wrote. A huge chunk of the surviving communication was addressed to Theo.

Until age 11, van Gogh attended a village school in Zundert, later transferring to a boarding school in Zevenbergen, where he was quite unhappy. At 13, he attended a secondary school in Tilburg. He performed well in academics, especially in language courses. For reasons unknown, he quit school in the middle of his second year and never returned. While he drew now and again, he wasn't a prodigy by any standard and displayed no extraordinary skills.

Art was something van Gogh landed upon by failing at other careers. He first worked at an art dealership in 1869 at The Hague, later moving to London and Paris for it. While stationed at London, he visited the iconic British Museum and National Gallery, among other famous institutions, to admire the artwork. He was fond of literature and read whatever he had access to, including museum guides. While the dealership exposed him to the top artists of the day, he did not enjoy the job profile he was given, and the differences led to him being dismissed in 1876. He then briefly taught at a boys' boarding school and a private school in England. In 1877, he went on to work in a bookshop, but that didn't last either. Over the years, his interest in religion had grown. He began fostering hope of entering the ministry, and his father supported his decision. However, van Gogh struggled with his theological studies and quit after a while. Still wishing to serve, he became a lay preacher in a Belgian mining community in 1879. He felt for the poor and the sick and distributed many of his possessions among them. But he failed in having his contract renewed and once again found himself without work. By this point, he had been sketching for some time. After short stints in such drastically different careers, it was upon Theo's encouragement that van Gogh decided to seriously pursue art at the age of 27.

In late 1880, van Gogh cultivated his drawing technique in Brussels. Since he had no earnings, he survived on the money Theo sent. A few months later, van Gogh moved back in with his parents, who were disappointed at this turn in his career. For them, becoming an artist was equivalent to failing in the eyes of society. What really pushed it over the edge for them was van Gogh's falling in love with his widowed cousin, a love that was not reciprocated by her nor its pursuit approved by his family. It led to a quarrel between the father and son, as a result of which van Gogh left home at Christmastime. He relocated to The Hague, then travelled ahead, and Theo continued supporting his brother, emotionally and financially. Although van Gogh took some painting lessons, he was largely self-taught. He referred to books on techniques, anatomy and perspectives, and copied his favourite works by the masters. At first, van Gogh preferred darker colours and depicting farmers and labourers in a rural setting. His most famous piece from this phase is *The Potato Eaters.* He hoped to send these paintings to Theo in exchange for the monetary support he lent, with the idea that Theo could sell them in Paris, but it was not to be. The dark tones were antithetical to the bright colours that were in trend in the city.

It was only in the second half of the 1880s that van Gogh began experimenting with brighter shades. He moved to Paris in 1886, where Theo introduced his brother to Impressionists such as Claude Monet who used vivid colours. Along with the palette, the setting and theme changed as his focus shifted to urban boulevards and cafés. He ultimately tired of the busy city life and retired to the French countryside in 1888. With the hope of setting up an artists' colony, he rented four rooms in the 'Yellow House' in the small town of Arles.

From this time onwards, van Gogh coped with mental health issues. He suffered from 'attacks', which his doctor diagnosed as a form of epilepsy. His treatment wasn't adequate by today's standards, considering the advancements that have been made in mental health support and knowledge. The incident he is most notorious for is cutting off a part of his left ear during one such attack in December 1888 after a fight with his artist-friend Paul Gauguin, whom van Gogh supposedly threatened with a razor. Gauguin was unharmed, but the police later found van Gogh in the bedroom, his ear mutilated and a pool of blood surrounding his unconscious body. They took him to a local hospital, where he was placed in an isolation cell. He was discharged in January 1889, but when he wasn't struggling with insomnia, he had nightmares. He admitted himself to a psychiatric hospital in Saint-Rémy in May, where he stayed for a year. Sadly, his mental illness eventually led him to commit suicide in 1890. On 27 July, he went to a nearby field to reportedly paint but shot himself with a revolver. He did not die on the spot; he managed to walk back to his room, where Theo cared for his brother for two days until he breathed his last.

In totality, van Gogh produced more than 2,000 artworks, a mix of oil paintings, watercolours, sketches and drawings—a gobsmacking number for any artist who has worked their entire life, but it's even more astounding when we realize that van Gogh's art career only spanned a decade. Why is he considered a failure-turned-success story then? Plainly seen, while he was respected in his own art circles near the end, he wasn't a commercially successful artist in his lifetime. It is the stuff of legend that he only ever sold a single painting and was reviewed by just one art critic (though he did receive nothing but praise from the said critic) while he was alive. He was also riddled with doubt regarding his skill. This made him an uncomfortable recipient of compliments, and the fact that he rarely sold his pieces made him continuously question his worth. A crossroads kept reappearing in his journey as an artist, and two choices were laid out for him:

Path 1

Like a virus, doubt crept upon van Gogh and infected him day and night. It whispered in his ears: he was a failure, yet again. While people smiled and complimented him, none of his art exhibitions translated into sales. There had been no monetary return, so he should give up on art and move to another type of work. It wasn't a big deal; he had done it before. Perhaps, he could swallow his distaste for the old art dealership and rejoin that organization. Or, he could take another gander at his religious studies, although his faith had evolved over the years and no longer aligned with the Church's beliefs.

Path 2

A huge gap lay between when van Gogh first attempted other occupations and his present self—he had already tried those career options before and knew for certain that none of them gave him joy, not the way creating art did. For the first time in his life, he found work that was more akin to a true vocation, indeed a calling, rather than a means of earning his livelihood. So, he stuck it out. He practised round-the-clock because even through mistakes, he improved a skill he was *passionate* about. Painting was his way of interpreting and connecting to the world, and he found something pure in it—joy.

The one thing that sustained van Gogh through all the hard times until his tragic death was the love he bore his art. Even when he was hospitalized for hurting his ear, he painted a self-portrait of his bandaged head, which is one of his most honest, captivating pieces. In the asylum, the attacks at times lasted days, and he could not muster up the energy to work. What was worse, during those attacks he sometimes attempted to eat poisonous paint, so he had to be prohibited from his studio. But art was what he returned to each time he felt better. It was his solace and gave his life purpose. As a matter of fact, he painted some of his most well-known artworks while he was in the asylum, at times looking out from barred windows, other times painting in the grounds.

After his death, Theo wanted to raise his brother's profile in the art world, but Theo passed away six months after van Gogh. Theo's widow, Jo van Gogh-Bonger, took up the task to fulfil her late husband's wishes. She promoted van Gogh's paintings by loaning them to museums and selling them. Her stroke of genius lay in the act of publishing van Gogh's letters to Theo in 1914. One of the reasons van Gogh's reputation as a 'tortured artist' still exists today is because he first gained fame for his arresting life story.

LASTING LESSON

We work for three reasons:
- to earn a livelihood,
- to be useful to others, or
- because we enjoy it.

Fortunate are those who are able to find the trio in their occupation, but most manage one or two. Without the usual driving force of earning money through his chosen career, van Gogh continued it because it gave him joy. We spend half of our adult lives at our jobs. Wouldn't it be better to do something we liked? Those who enjoy what they do are more likely to persevere through tough times as well. We can all be cogs in a machine, repeating actions from nine in the morning to five in the evening, but what can separate us from others is the pleasure we take in our occupations and the resulting curiosity to learn and improve.

This is the ideal scenario though. Due to our circumstances, many of us are forced into jobs that may not thrill us. And even if we do have an exciting one, we need to do tasks every day that are necessary but may not be fun, such as household chores. Another form of the lesson can be applied in those scenarios, one that affects our attitude regarding work—if it doesn't give us joy, we should search for ways to *make* it enjoyable. In case someone despises cleaning their house, they could turn on some music and sing and dance their way around while completing the errand. If another wishes to improve their health but doesn't like exercising, they could attempt activities that suit their pace, whether it's yoga in a park, dance lessons or a sport, since not everyone has to go to the gym. We'll find ourselves doing tasks quicker and, more importantly, *wanting* to do them once we:

FIND JOY IN WORK.

Vincent and Vincent

While Vincent van Gogh was the oldest surviving child of his parents, he wasn't their firstborn. His mother had delivered a stillborn baby also named Vincent exactly a year before van Gogh's birth, that is, 30 March 1852. It is said that van Gogh walked past a tombstone bearing his name daily due to the first Vincent's death.

NOTHING CAN REPLACE HARD WORK AND PERSEVERANCE

Thomas Edison (1847–1931)

Inventor

Genius is 1 per cent inspiration and 99 per cent perspiration.

Thomas Edison

O
ften dubbed the most influential inventor of the past millennium, Thomas Edison changed what people thought were the limits of their senses. He's considered a controversial figure, especially due to his dealings with Nikola Tesla, but there can be no doubt that Edison made massive contributions to science and technology. He amassed over 2,000 patents in his lifetime, and some of the things we take for granted today exist because he converted ideas into usable technologies. Born in an era in which electricity was a novelty, he left the world filled with cities glittering with electrical force. This was all thanks to not just his invention of the incandescent light bulb but the setting up of the first commercial power grid as well. The Wizard of Menlo Park, as he was fondly called, was an astute businessman and knew how to market himself and his products through the public persona he had created. Organizations that he

helped create are in operation even today. In fact, Edison's own electric company merged with its competitor to form General Electric Company in 1892, popularly known as GE these days. Almost a decade prior to this, Edison, along with others such as Alexander Graham Bell, founded the largest technical professional organization, the Institute of Electrical and Electronics Engineers (IEEE), which awards a medal in Edison's name right to this day.

While Edison was gifted, nothing was handed to him on a platter, silver or otherwise. He was a notoriously hard worker, and the invention that put him on the map was the fruit of tireless hours and thousands of flopped experiments. What kept his spirit alive through countless failures was his attitude, for which the world will forever be grateful to him.

THE MAN IN THE WIZARD'S HAT

On 11 February 1847, Thomas Alva Edison was born as the seventh child of Nancy and Samuel in Ohio, United States. He was among the couple's four children who witnessed adulthood. The family moved to Port Huron in Michigan when he was seven. Edison's father dipped his toe in a variety of trades, including carpentry and farming. Although Edison came from modest beginnings, his family wasn't poor by any means: he always had good food on the table and books to read.

Edison had always been inquisitive. As a kid, he sat on a goose's eggs to see if he could hatch them—it might very well have been his first experiment and a failed one at that. He started schooling in Michigan where his teachers found his constant questions exasperating. Having been a former educator, his mother decided to homeschool him herself so that she could craft the courses according to his curiosity and intelligence. At age 12, he wanted to venture out into the world that lay wide open for him due to the new Grand Trunk Railroad criss-crossing the country. He got a job selling newspapers and sweets on a daily route running between Port Huron and Detroit. With the money he earned, he built himself a small chemical laboratory in a corner of the baggage car. Two years into this occupation, he became interested in the process of printing, so he began his own press and published the first-ever newspaper on a train, *The Weekly Herald.* It was filled with local news and gossip, business facts and even some philosophical thoughts of his own. Unfortunately, he faced two accidents in this period. He became partially deaf, which was not uncommon at the time in young folk because of the lack of antibiotics. And at age 16, he accidentally set fire to the baggage car with his chemicals, due to which the conductor chucked him out along with all of his science experiments. But every rainstorm brings in its wake a clear blue sky. Reportedly, Edison saved the life of a young boy who had walked in front of a moving train. The boy's father, a telegraph operator, taught Edison the techniques of telegraphy as a reward. The age's fastest way of long-distance communication aptly required quick thinking and reflexes, which Edison soon mastered.

For the next four years, Edison became a wandering telegraph operator, never settling down in one place for long. He claimed the deafness helped his career as it left him no choice but to focus on his machine in the surrounding thrum of tapping needles. Since the operators had to maintain their equipment, he gained practical knowledge about electricity on the job. It furthered his curiosity about the subject. In 1869, Edison registered his first patent, that of an electrical vote recorder, only to find that politicians didn't want to quicken the process. This failure taught him early on to cater to the public.

In 1871, Edison married Mary Stillwell, with whom he had three children (fondly calling the oldest two 'Dot' and 'Dash' after the marks used in Morse code). Three years later, he sold the improvements he had made to the telegraph and took the earnings to establish the first industrial-scale research laboratory, 'The Invention Factory', and became a full-time inventor in Menlo Park.

Edison filled his lab with the best equipment and technicians that money could procure, and decided to produce a minor invention every month and a major one every six months. A hardworking man, he spent more time in his laboratory than at home. He was also competitive, so much so that he was upset he didn't come up with the telephone, though he did invent a carbon transmitter that improved the sound quality of the device. In 1877, he was tinkering with the repeating telegraph, an invention of his that automatically took down messages for relay. The telegraph made indentations on a sheet of thick paper that spun around a needle. On this particular day, it began spinning out of control and emitted a strange sound that gave him the idea of the phonograph—a device that could record sound and play it back, the device we have to thank for all of our music players and speakers. The phonograph became a hit. At 31, he was invited to The White House to demonstrate the machine for the president. With such feats to boast of, Edison became the golden boy of the press and utilized it to build up his image as 'the inventor.' He deliberately chose to be absent when the press entered his lab and glided into the room from a corner with smudges on his face and perspiration lining his forehead. Enamoured by this mysterious genius, the press would be further charmed by his sense of humour.

By the late 1870s, Edison became preoccupied with an exercise that many had attempted but failed at—inventing the incandescent light bulb. It had been patented decades earlier, but a viable mechanism hadn't yet been devised. Homes used candles or gas lights. Both were fire risks and the latter could lead to asphyxiation too, due to which inventors wished to create safer and cleaner sources of light. In 1878, Edison announced that he would unveil his light bulb in a few days' time. On the basis of just that announcement, all sorts of financiers wound up at his door to invest in what would be the next big thing. Edison further vowed that within a few weeks, he would set Lower Manhattan aglow with incandescent light. Weeks turned to months, and the months became a year. The press began losing their faith in Edison and called him a 'quack', while his investors turned uneasy as nothing happened, or so it seemed to the outside world. Inside Menlo Park, however, Edison struggled with not only finding the perfect filament that would give a steady glow for long durations without burning out, but also with the task of setting up an infrastructure that would support the bulb. And so he reached his crossroads:

Path 1
This position wasn't unfamiliar to Edison. He'd tried to invent things that no one else had thought of or come close to executing. And after many failed attempts, he realized it

was time to give up. This incandescent bulb was becoming an embarrassment and beginning to undermine the public persona he had toiled to create. Fame, that fickle thing, and his reputation, were what enabled him to reach out to big-time investors. If he lost access to them, how would he proceed? And he had scores of other ideas that he could work on; perhaps, even go back to his phonograph and adapt it for commercial use. That would surely shut everyone up.

Path 2

Anyone could come up with ideas, but what separated paper drawings from a working product was dedication. The spirit of invention required sacrifice in the shape of long hours spent on botched attempts that were never to be regarded as failures. The true inventor used each misstep to shortlist the ways to make a machine function. If Edison had let the prospect of failure overwhelm him, he wouldn't have invented anything since hardly anything worked in its first test run.

Through trial and error with various inorganic and organic materials, Edison and his team finally discovered that carbon was the perfect filament. On New Year's Eve 1879, hundreds travelled to Menlo Park by train to find the structure illuminated by bulbs of the kind they had never seen before. However, that didn't complete the task. Many assume that creating electric light was as straightforward as making the bulb. What they forget is that the bulb had to be fitted into a socket, which had to be connected to electric wires in a metred system and further attached to an electric power grid. None of these elements existed at the time. The inventor became a businessman as he established the Edison Electric Light Company that provided this setup. He even had to convince New York City officials that power lines beneath the city wouldn't be harmful (we must remember that this was an entirely new concept at the time). Finally, in September 1882, four years late to his promise, Edison and his team flipped the switch to deliver power to the first district in Manhattan. While he is most famous for inventing the light bulb, his other contributions were by no means pale in comparison. He built the first motion-picture camera, called the kinetograph, and its viewing instrument, the kinetoscope. He also conceived of the alkaline storage battery.

Two years after the death of his first wife, Edison married Mina Miller, whom he reportedly proposed to in Morse code. They went on to have three children. He passed away at the age of 84 on 18 October 1931, leaving behind a bright legacy. More than 50,000 people paid their respects, and on the third night, upon the president's request, radio listeners across the country switched off their lights as a reminder of what the earth would have been like without Thomas Edison.

LASTING LESSON

There are no shortcuts in life. Granted, certain bents of mind and smarter ways to work can aid a process, but any large goal requires discipline and perseverance. Each day sees the development of new technology that makes our tasks easier. On the flip side, it makes us lazier and our attention spans shorter. We're living in an age in which we're constantly bombarded with multimedia content and world leaders can express their thoughts globally and instantaneously in 280 characters. Of course, if Edison were alive today, he would have had much more technical support to conduct his experiments. But whatever he came up with was revolutionary, and anything out of the ordinary requires that much extra effort. Anyone attempting projects of similar calibre would have to stick it out too through multiple failed tries.

The spirit of hard work might have even come easier to Edison, who was used to toiling from a young age, whereas we're in the era of instant gratification today. However, certain aims will always take longer and require determination—whether it's learning an instrument or a new language, settling into an alien atmosphere, or inventing something extraordinary. Being mindful of the scale of work involved can warn us so that we are not disoriented whenever we chance upon obstacles, but such preparation isn't always possible either. When we do come across hurdles, we have to leap over them while keeping our eyes set on the final goal. It's no lie that anything worth achieving requires exertion. And the more effort we put in, the sweeter the reward shall be, which we can all taste if we remember that:

NOTHING CAN REPLACE HARD WORK AND PERSEVERANCE.

Triumphant Thomas

Edison had a wager going with other workers in Menlo Park over whether the phonograph would work or not. The prize? Fifteen cigars. His employees gathered around him as he inserted a sheet of tin foil, attached a mouthpiece and recited the nursery rhyme, 'Mary Had a Little Lamb'. Once he played the device, it spoke back to him in his own voice, repeating the rhyme. Before this contraption, sound had been ephemeral, something that could not be captured for posterity's sake. Edison made sound concrete and won a bet in the process.

DO NOT FEAR FAILURE

Julia Child (1912–2004)

Cookbook author and TV personality

If you're going to have a sense of fear of failure, you're just never going to learn how to cook because cooking is—well, lots of it is—one failure after another, and that's how you finally learn.

Julia Child

Here is a legend who was awarded the American Presidential Medal of Freedom, was inducted as a Chevalier in France's Legion of Honour and worked for the precursor to the Central Intelligence Agency (CIA) during World War II. However, what she's best known for is having been a cookbook author and TV personality. In her 91 years, Julia Child lived a full, fascinating life. She resided and worked in different parts of the world, including Sri Lanka, China, France, Germany and Norway. She brought French cooking to the United States and revealed the secrets of the technical—and at times intimidating—cuisine to the masses. Her sparkling wit and pleasing persona made her a frequent guest on talk shows as a celebrity chef, and she hosted cooking shows of her own across a period of almost 40 years. For these, she won the Emmy and Peabody awards. In addition to this, she was also the bestselling author of more than a dozen cookbooks, and those interested in French cuisine refer to her recipes even today. Several educational institutions, such as Brown University, Smith College, Rutgers University and Harvard University, presented her with honorary doctorates. And she made history by becoming the first woman to be inducted into The Culinary Institute of America's Hall of Fame. Here's another fancy credit to boot: Meryl Streep portrayed her in the movie *Julie & Julia*.

Contrary to cooking shows today in which each ingredient is meticulously measured and laid out and every recipe immaculately executed, Child regularly made mistakes on her shows. Her attitude regarding failures in the kitchen allowed her to manoeuvre situations that could have turned incredibly awkward. It also made her goof-ups endearing and a part of her charm that oozed off the screen, making her such a relatable and legendary TV star.

THE WOMAN BEHIND THE COOKING COUNTER

Julia Child was born as Julia Carolyn McWilliams on 15 August 1912 in California, US, in a well-to-do family. She was the eldest of three children, having one brother and sister. Child was named after her mother, an heir to a paper company fortune. Child's father, John McWilliams, managed agricultural land and was involved in real estate. She thus grew up in a wealthy household brimming with parties and unsurprisingly never felt the need to cook.

Upon completing her schooling, Child attended the all-women's Smith College at the age of 18. At 6'2", she held a formidable presence on the basketball court and excelled at the sport. She graduated after four years with a Bachelor's degree in history but to the consternation of most, as a *bachelorette* herself, since women were expected to find husbands at college in those days. As a fashionable member of a well-known family, Child was quite the socialite. She had plans of being a novelist, though nothing ever became of it. She applied for roles at magazines but wasn't offered any. After a year, she found herself restless and moved to New York City to work as a copywriter for an upscale furniture store. She found her way back to her parents' home in Pasadena in 1937 and floated around from one job to another as she wasn't entirely sure what to make of her career. Meanwhile, her social life provided her the entertainment she desired.

The never-ending party did finally break with the US joining World War II in 1942. Child, now 30, wanted to aid the war effort but discovered she was too tall for the women's defence forces. She began working for a government information agency in Washington DC as a secretary. A few months later, she moved to the Office of Strategic Services (OSS), which would eventually become the CIA. Although she was akin to a research assistant, it was here that she dabbled with her first recipe. She worked on something that sounds right out of a spy film—a *shark repellent*—a version of which is still used today. In 1944, she set out on her first overseas mission to Ceylon, as Sri Lanka was known back then, and served as the OSS Registry Chief. To an outsider, her life may seem to have been turned upside down as she was now forced to live in small quarters in a foreign land where nobody knew who her family was. But she was thrilled with the adventure. It's also how she met Paul Child, who had moved from his previous post at Delhi to head the OSS's

Visual Presentation group in Sri Lanka. Ten years senior and a few inches shorter to her, he carried with him a sense of urbane sophistication. Fond of gourmet food, he was an artist and photographer and fluent in several languages, including French. Both were transferred to China, where Paul introduced her to the local cuisine. They moved back to the US after the war to their respective hometowns but were married a year later. Paul's job was absorbed into the State Department, so the couple lived in Washington DC for the next two years. In 1948, he received an overseas assignment in Paris, France. Little did Child know that this would kick off a new phase in her life.

Child instantly fell in love with Paris and its food. She enrolled at the French cooking school, Le Cordon Bleu, and was the lone woman in her class. She earned her diploma in 1951 after *failing* the exam the previous year. At almost 40, she'd finally struck upon something she felt passionate about. Along with two friends, Child began a cooking school, L'École des Trois Gourmandes, or The School of the Three Hearty Eaters. The trio of hearty eaters also started researching, testing and writing recipes for what would become the revolutionary cookbook, *Mastering the Art of French Cooking*. Child felt strongly about it being a proper teaching book for novice cooks as opposed to a collection of recipes in which the steps weren't fully explained. It would take nine years before they completed and published their project, which was rejected by publishers until it landed on the desk of an editor at Alfred A. Knopf. In the meantime, Paul got reassigned to Marseilles and Child discovered the differences between regional cooking and the one she'd learnt in the capital city. They later moved to Germany,

Norway and then back to Washington DC in 1960. Through it all, French cuisine remained her favourite.

Child published her first cookbook, a tome at almost 700 pages, at the age of 49. She appeared on talk shows to promote the book, and her effervescence and ease in front of the camera caught everyone's eyes. Soon, she was offered her own cooking show, *The French Chef*, though she was neither of the two—French or a professional chef. Thus, she started her TV career at the age of 50 and was an instant hit, loved by all. She went on to pen more cookbooks, star in more shows of her own and make appearances in those hosted by others. In one such stint on *Late Night with David Letterman* in 1987, in which she was supposed to teach the viewers how to make the perfect burger patty, she found the main equipment faulty while the clock of her short segment kept ticking away. That's how, in front of a live studio audience of a popular TV show, Child discovered a crossroads:

Path 1

Child wasn't on the show to cook a complicated recipe. She'd been a household name for over 20 years, and the crew couldn't manage to get her the bare essentials—a working burner! It was so embarrassing though none of it was her fault. But the viewers at home would associate the failure of the recipe with *her* because she wasn't delivering what she had promised. She should ask the crew to stop filming while they fixed their mess. She had come in especially for this segment, and she was going to proceed according to the set plan.

Path 2

The one thing the kitchen had taught Child was that accidents happen. Whether it was broken appliances or personal errors—it was all part of the process. If she had ever let the idea of cooking mistakes daunt her, she would never have been able to feel at ease in the kitchen, *especially* in front of a filming crew. This was a good TV spot, but it was just one opportunity and it didn't define her or her overall success. All she could do was laugh, crack jokes and make the best of a bad situation.

Without missing a beat, Child used the raw meat and ingredients on the table to make a tartare, using a blow torch to melt the cheese on top. She accompanied it with a smile on her face and quips to elicit laughter from the audience. It was by no means a classic tartare recipe, but the ease and confidence with which she executed and tasted it, anyone would have been tempted to try it for themselves. This was a signature Julia Child move—in all her shows, she made mistakes in the kitchen, such as not flipping a potato pancake right and having to put the fallen pieces back together. She would ask the viewers that if no one in the kitchen was around to see the mistake, how did it matter? Well, *she* had thousands of people peeking into her kitchen, but that didn't detract her from knocking over cutlery, banging utensils or dropping food and laughing it off. In fact, if she noticed a small mistake she had made, which an amateur at home couldn't have, she pointed it out and informed her viewers of the correct procedure. Instead of losing people's trust in her cooking skills, this trait of hers endeared her to the masses. They realized it was okay to experiment in the kitchen and not always be perfect.

Child continued working into her late eighties. She donated her kitchen—which formed the set of her cooking shows—to the Smithsonian, where it can be viewed even today. In 1991, she helped launch a Master of Liberal Arts in Gastronomy at Boston University so that other Americans could access the kind of training she had received in Paris. She also set up The Julia Child Foundation for Gastronomy and the Culinary Arts in 1995 to support others interested in the field. She passed away on 13 August 2004, just two days short of her ninety-second birthday.

LASTING LESSON

It is a fact of life—we are all going to fail. We fail at everyday tasks, we fail at short-term goals and we may fail at achieving lifelong aspirations. In our entire lives, we set out to accomplish millions and millions of targets, and there is no way that we will always be greeted with success. While we should aim high, we should be prepared for crash landings. What can help cushion the blow is prioritizing our tasks so that we can devote our limited energy to projects accordingly. Even if we give something we want our very best, there's always a chance we won't prevail. There are over seven billion people on this planet. While there may be ample opportunities, as we climb the ladder and enter niche spaces, the coveted spots grow smaller in number. There will probably be someone out there who can not only offer what we have to bring to the table, but perhaps outperform us as well. Once we stop placing the notion of our ideal selves on a pedestal and see what we truly are—human beings with flaws—we will learn to accept our losses better. And this attitude will help us deal with our everyday blunders as well, whether we are late to meet a friend, leave milk on the stove for too long or forget someone's birthday. This is not to say that we shouldn't hold ourselves accountable for our mishaps—the sole way to improve is by learning from our mistakes—but we shouldn't beat ourselves up or stay awake at night thinking of all the faux pas we've ever committed. It's great to strive for perfection, but it will only prove harmful if we never accept anything less. This shouldn't stop us from trying at all, because success is impossible for someone who doesn't make an attempt. So, take that step ahead, hoping for optimum results, but:

DO NOT FEAR FAILURE.

Child's Cats

There are several biographies about Julia Child, and one also bases it around her love for cats. Her adoration of the feline species supposedly began in France when a little kitten walked into her kitchen. The cat that the couple adopted became a favourite topic to discuss in letters to family. Paul even entered a jovial competition with his brother to compare their cats' inquisitiveness. Child reportedly named all of her cats either Minette or Minou (French for female and male cat, respectively), as was the fashion in France. In 2004, her little Minou lay curled up next to her on the bed as Child went to sleep for the very last time.

NO WORK IS SMALL WORK

Dr. Seuss (1904–1991)

Children's author

I know my stuff looks like it was all rattled off in 28 seconds, but every word is a struggle and every sentence is like the pangs of birth.

Dr. Seuss

Upon hearing the words 'cultural icon' and 'Pulitzer Prize winner', we may not immediately conjure up the image of a children's author. But both terms correctly describe Theodor Geisel, or the man popularly known as Dr. Seuss. He published over 40 books in his lifetime, which have sold more than 600 million copies worldwide, beating sales of the likes of J.K. Rowling and R.L. Stine. Some of his famous works include *The Cat in the Hat*, *Green Eggs and Ham* and *Horton Hears a Who*. While he was from the United States, Geisel's books haven't been exclusively enjoyed by the young readers of just that country. His writing has been translated to over 20 languages, including Spanish, Dutch, German, Yiddish and even Latin. Moreover, they're devoured by people across all ages. Several books of his have been turned to popular films, such as *How the Grinch Stole Christmas*, starring Jim Carrey. Apart from being a beloved author who shaped many a childhood, he was an artist, political cartoonist, animator and filmmaker, having won the Academy Award for Best Documentary Feature too. He was also awarded the Legion of Merit for his service to the US military in World War II, during which he wrote and directed films to uplift the soldiers' morale.

Yet, Geisel didn't always know how his legacy would unfold. For the better part of his earlier years, he had 'loftier' goals in mind, but they never came to pass. How he changed his outlook towards his career stands as a lesson for us all.

GEISEL BEFORE SEUSS

Theodor Seuss Geisel was born on 2 March 1904 in Massachusetts, US, to parents with German roots. His father Theodor Robert Geisel worked at Kuhlmbach & Geisel, the brewery that his own father had set up and one which was (perhaps aptly) referred to as 'Come back and guzzle' in local taverns. The 'Seuss' in Geisel's name came from his mother Henrietta's maiden name.

A shy boy, Geisel preferred the company of close-knit companions. At the top of this list was his elder sister Marnie. The two would often play in the nearby Forest Park, which even had a zoo. Their father took them to the zoo every Sunday, where a fascinated Geisel sketched the animals. His mother encouraged his artistic tendencies and allowed him to draw animal caricatures on the walls of his bedroom. Every night, she read the children rhyming books from two languages, which instilled in Geisel a love for rhythm and cadence. His idyllic childhood left a lasting impression, but once the US entered World War I, anti-German sentiment spread throughout the country. Later, with the Prohibition (the nationwide ban of alcohol in the US, 1919–1933), the family brewery was forced shut. But the family's association with it and Geisel's ancestry still made him an easy target for schoolmates' jibes. He didn't perform exceptionally well at school but still made his way into the Ivy League Dartmouth College in 1921. His interest was captured by the college's humour magazine, *The Dartmouth Jack-O-Lantern*. Here, he found a haven to write rhymes and draw fantastical creatures. He eventually became its editor-in-chief. However, he was officially removed from the magazine when he and his friends were caught with a pint of bootleg gin during Prohibition. Curiously, the number of illustrations by several new strange-named artists increased in the magazine that year, with submissions from L. Pasteur and D.G. Rossetti (like the long-dead chemist Louis Pasteur and poet Dante Gabriel Rossetti, respectively) and even a Seuss. This was the first time that Geisel had used his middle name to sign off one of his artworks. After his graduation in 1925, in which his classmates reportedly voted him 'Least Likely to Succeed', he went to Oxford to pursue a PhD in English literature that he would never complete. It was fortuitous he went because through it he met the person who pushed him to professionally pursue art.

Geisel found his thoughts drifting in tedious lectures that analysed the punctuation used in Shakespearean plays, and he killed time by drawing creatures on the margins of his notebooks. A fellow student Helen Palmer noted them and inquired why he was wasting his time in class when he was obviously destined for something else. He grew fond of her and finally heeded her advice. He dropped out of university, dashing his father's dream of Geisel earning a doctorate, and travelled across Europe in 1926. He returned to the US the following year, moved back in with his parents and tried to become self-sufficient by submitting cartoons to national magazines. Finally, one got accepted for publication, which he had submitted under 'Seuss', hoping to reserve his full name for more 'serious' and 'literary' pursuits, like the Great American Novel. He had finished writing it during his travels through Europe, only to realize later that it wasn't actually that great. He cut it into a short story, which wasn't particularly brilliant either, then reduced it further to a two-line joke that he finally sold to a magazine.

Meanwhile, with the confidence boost that the cartoon publication granted Geisel, he moved to New York City to play in the big leagues. All he seemed to get were rejections, until he finally heard of an old classmate working at *Judge* magazine, who in turn introduced Geisel to its editor. Geisel was hired as a writer–artist, thus receiving the cushion he needed to marry Palmer. During this time, he added the 'Dr.' in front of 'Seuss' to sound more professorial and make up for the doctorate he didn't achieve. Four months into the job, he drew a cartoon depicting a knight who had been rudely awakened by a roaring dragon. It contained the line, 'Darn it all, another Dragon, and just after I'd sprayed the whole castle with Flit!' The people at Flit, a popular bug spray of the time, saw its advertising potential and stole Geisel away. He created ad campaigns for the company for over 15 years. While he continued submitting to magazines, his contract with the makers of Flit forbade him from most avenues. As the bug spray required seasonal work, he had a lot of time on his hands and not many options to pursue. But he discovered a loophole—there were no restrictions on writing children's books. On a 1937 stormy voyage across the Atlantic, he found himself stringing words along to the beat of the engines about a street from his childhood. Six months later, it became *And to Think That I Saw It on Mulberry Street*. It was rejected by 27 publishers. Geisel was close to burning the manuscript when he ran into an acquaintance from Dartmouth, who had been appointed editor at a publishing house that very day and signed the book on. The sales were modest, though famed author Beatrix Potter praised it. The success of his first children's book was bittersweet for Geisel because the person who had made him fall in love with words, his mother, had passed away in 1931.

Geisel tried breaking into the adult books market in 1939 with *The Seven Lady Godivas*, but it flopped. The same year, he hoped his invention of an 'Infantograph', which could predict what a couple's biological children would look like, would be a sweet cash cow. Alas, he never perfected the technology. He wrote other books, but his 1940 *Horton Hatches the Egg* was his last for seven years as he began working for a liberal newspaper, *PM*. Too old to fight in World War II, he joined Frank Capra's documentary unit, writing and directing animated films to train and entertain the army. After the war, Geisel made another attempt at a large juicy project—he ventured into Hollywood. He worked on a live-action musical fantasy called *The 5,000 Fingers of Dr. T*. Like several other attempts at distinguished success, it was a failure, pushing Geisel to a crossroads:

Path 1

Geisel had been reserving his full name 'Theodor Seuss Geisel' for something big—something that would leave a mark in the history books. And he'd been trying so hard! It wasn't like he had restricted himself to a single field. No, no, he had kept his options open, hoping to strike gold wherever he could. But his 'great literary novel' literally became a piece of joke, his illustrated book for adults was a bust, his foray into technology didn't yield any fruit and his Hollywood movie tanked at the box office. He had to try something else, because he refused to be *stuck* writing children's books his entire life.

Path 2

Through it all, Geisel had succeeded under his silly pseudonym—Dr. Seuss. The goofy drawings that Dr. Seuss made, whether for ad agencies or children, were a huge hit. But he was perceived as either 'selling out' or doing simple tasks, though they were anything but. Just because the book had fewer words, it did not mean writing it was an elementary exercise that could be completed in a few days. *He* knew how much work went into illustrating and writing stories for young readers... and perhaps that should be enough?

While Geisel published his first children's book in 1937, he would only gradually grow into the role of a writer that influenced young minds. After the war, baby boomers reached the age of joining school while their parents entered a phase of unexpected prosperity. They wished to and could afford to send their children to university, but therein lay a problem—the children couldn't read. In the mid-1950s, the issue of high illiteracy in the US entered public discussion, and Geisel was challenged by a publishing friend to write a primer for children that would engage them while aiding their reading capabilities. For this, Geisel had to come up with an exciting story that used about 200 different words— what an impediment for someone who came up with new words and odd names for his creatures, and wrote them all in rhyme! He tried various combinations and was close to giving up on the project when he landed on the cat–hat rhyme, and the resulting 1957 *The Cat in the Hat* revolutionized children's education.

Geisel soon became a household name, his royalties increasing from $5,000 a year to about $200,000 in 1959. With his wife and a friend, Geisel went on to launch Beginner Books, a new publishing business that focused on creating fun primers that kids actually wanted to read. He laboured close to eight hours every day on his books, writing, rewriting and then rewriting some more. To create a 60-page book, he would often produce a thousand pages, until he felt he had perfected it. In 1955, the 'Dr.' in his pen name was legitimized by his old college, Dartmouth, as he was presented with an honorary doctorate. His wife Palmer died in 1967, and a year later he married his second wife, Audrey Stone. He did not father children with her either, though he was stepdad to Stone's two kids. He worked well into his last years, his farewell book being the 1990 *Oh, the Places You'll Go*, which is even today a popular gift for graduating students. He passed away on 24 September 1991 at the age of 87, but his parting words to the world remained at the top of the bestsellers list for a whole year afterwards.

LASTING LESSON

Every career gets ascribed a value—some are considered more noble pursuits, others frivolous. Some more challenging, others an easy way out. These set standards leave no room for a person's own interests to bloom. The trends change from community to community. Largely in India, subjects and trades related to the sciences, business and law are seen as more attractive and lucrative, while the arts are looked down upon. Indeed, many schools stop children from pursuing the science stream in classes eleventh and twelfth if they haven't scored high in prior years, discounting the child's own area of interest. And if a child who scores well wishes to pursue the arts, they are talked out of it. There is, of course, a supposed rationale behind this—certain careers seem to have better pay and job security than others (although in today's time where MBA degrees have become so common, the competition in these fields is cutthroat too). Parents want the best for their children, but this kind of thinking doesn't take into account how much priority their kids would eventually give to their earnings and how much to their passions. One could earn a lot yet be deeply dissatisfied with their work because they find it a drudgery. Such a way of thinking also feeds into the class system in India, attributing respect to certain sections of society while treating others with disdain. These societal norms aren't restricted to careers but apply to women's choices as well. Some criticize women for being homemakers and 'wasted resources', while others for working and thus 'ignoring their families'—there really is no winning in such situations.

Since we don't operate in a vacuum, such external

voices pervade our thinking and impact the way we view ourselves. Due to this, many ignore their own instincts and desires because they don't fit into what our society deems as valuable or ideal. Albeit, the sole constant we have in life is ourselves, and we have to ultimately be at peace with our decisions. Shouldn't we choose what makes us happy instead of pacifying those around us? All we have to do is respect each individual's choice, which we can do by giving due credit for the effort that goes behind the scenes that we may not always be aware of, because:

NO WORK IS SMALL WORK.

Seuss's Silliness

Although shy around strangers, Seuss had to attend events due to his celebrity status. He disappeared at one such party, only to be later found in the host's library, signing books as R.L. Stevenson. He repeated his vanishing act at a charity ball being hosted in a department store and was later tracked to the women's section, reducing the prices of designer shoes. His reason? He believed they were ridiculously expensive!

SUCCESS REQUIRES SACRIFICE

Nelson Mandela (1918–2013)

Political activist and former President of
South Africa

*The ANC's vision of a South Africa in which people
live in peace and with equal opportunities is an ideal
which sustained me during the 27 years in prison. It is
an ideal for which I was prepared to sacrifice my life.*

Nelson Mandela

n times of suffering emerge courageous challengers of
authority who change the course of history—one such
man was Nelson Mandela. A lawyer, political activist and
philanthropist, Mandela fought against the racist Apartheid
regime of twentieth-century South Africa and spent nearly
three decades in prison for the cause. He became a symbol for
the oppressed citizens of an entire nation and helped abolish
Apartheid in the early nineties. In 1994, he became the first
Black president of the country in its first-ever democratic
elections, in which each individual—whatever the colour of
their skin—had one vote. After serving his five-year term,
he helped negotiate peace in other African nations and
established the charitable Nelson Mandela Foundation. In
his lifetime, he received close to 700 awards, including the

Bharat Ratna. He and former South African President Frederik Willem de Klerk were jointly awarded the Nobel Peace Prize in 1993 for putting their disagreements aside to peacefully transition to a nation that had a majority rule. Mandela also holds interesting connections to other personas in this book— he encouraged Oprah Winfrey to build a school for girls in South Africa and, in consultation with Sir Richard Branson, Mandela founded a collective of world leaders called The Elders, who tackle some of the globe's toughest problems.

Having grown up learning about the struggle for Indian Independence, we know that the life of a freedom fighter is anything but easy. Mandela dedicated himself to his people, often at the cost of other aspects of his identity. Yet he stated that if it had been required, he would have done it all over again.

THE MAN BEHIND THE SYMBOL

Mandela was born on 18 July 1918 in a small village in the then-Transkei region of South Africa to a family of royal lineage. His father Nkosi Mphakanyiswa Gadla Mandela, a tribal chief and counsellor to the king of the Thembu people, had four wives. One of them was Mandela's mother, Nonqaphi Fanny Nosekeni. Their son was named Rolihlahla at birth, which in Xhosa means 'pulling the branch of a tree' or 'troublemaker'—a sign of things to come for the White establishment.

All of the chief's children lived together, playing and at times fighting but ending each day by eating from one dish. A favourite pastime of the children was stick fighting, in which they parried oncoming blows with a stick in one hand as they used a stick in the other hand to strike at their opponent. Mandela helped around the house by looking after the sheep, goat, horses and cattle. The first in the family to attend school, he was sent to the local Methodist missionary one. On his first day there, he was given the Christian name Nelson by his teacher. Young Mandela told his mother, whom he dearly loved, about the new name, but she was unable to pronounce the alien language.

Having lost his father at a young age, Mandela was entrusted to the care of his uncle, King Jongintaba Dalindyebo. He raised the boy as his own, with the hope that Mandela would one day become chief counsellor to the king's son and heir, Justice Mtirara. Mandela thus grew up in the grandeur of the royal court. Awestruck, he observed the elders, who were experts in tribal customs and unafraid to criticize the king. This became Mandela's first interaction with a democracy. He performed errands for the elders and learnt a great deal in exchange—the history of his people, the times before the Europeans reached African shores and the clash of the Black people's spears against the Whites' gunpowder. As a part of his grooming, Mandela was sent to an elite boarding school and matriculated from another reputable institute. Displaying leadership qualities from an early age, he was appointed prefect in his second year at the institute. He also picked up the hobbies of boxing and long-distance running, to which he would later add ballroom dancing. With the king's blessing, Mandela went to the University of Fort Hare to pursue a Bachelor in Arts, hoping to become an interpreter or clerk in the Native Affairs Department. At the university, he met the man who would become his future colleague and lifelong friend, Oliver Tambo. However, Mandela couldn't complete his degree as he was expelled for participating in a student protest. When he returned home, he was told that the king had fixed marriages for both Mandela and Justice. The boys' reaction? They ran away.

The two arrived at Johannesburg, a big city unlike anything they had seen before, in 1941. The stratified society shocked Mandela. Black people weren't allowed to reside within the cities, so they poured in by the thousands from surrounding ghettoes to perform menial work for a pittance. Mandela himself began working as a security officer in the mines but was dismissed when it was discovered that he had run away and was needed back by his king. Among the smattering of Black businesspeople was the realtor Walter Sisulu. Mandela was fascinated by the fact that Sisulu ran his own business. Sisulu, in return, was impressed by the 23-year-old's commanding presence and wish to be a lawyer. Sisulu helped arrange a clerical job at a law firm for Mandela as he pursued his Bachelor's degree by correspondence from the University of South Africa, which he completed in 1943. Sisulu saw in Mandela the potential to become a leading force in the struggle and introduced the young man to the African National Congress (ANC), the oldest Black political party opposing White minority rule in South Africa. At the time, it favoured moderate means of protests, such as organizing boycotts and sending petitions and letters. Much like hearing the elders' exchange of ideas in his childhood, Mandela observed the party meetings and rarely spoke as he wasn't confident of his English-language skills. To support the Allies' effort in World War II, Black South Africans were put to work in factories in the name of freedom and equality—two things they were denied in their own land. But the ideals inspired Mandela to mobilize the masses for African nationalism, and to that effect he co-founded the ANC's Youth League in 1944. He was shy no more. That same year, he married Evelyn Ntoko Mase, a nurse, and had a child the following year, a son named Madiba Thembekile Mandela. For the first time in his life, Mandela had a home of his own.

In 1948, the White Afrikaners (descendants of mostly Dutch traders who had reached the continent in the seventeenth century) came into power with the National Party. While the Africans had also been mistreated earlier, the government now enshrined that attitude in law under the new Apartheid system that discriminated on the basis of race. Separate spaces were allocated to the Blacks, including toilets, schools, transport, beaches and park benches. They had no voting rights, were exiled to rural outposts and even required passes—a sort of ID booklet—to move around in public. These passes could be demanded to be seen at any point, and the failure to have one led to immediate arrest. In response, the ANC launched the Campaign for the Defiance of Unjust Laws, a non-violent civil disobedience act. Mandela organized support for the campaign and represented a shift to a more assertive, aggressive approach. The campaign's popularity made him a well-known figure around the country. As a result, the government took out a banning order in 1952 that severely restricted his freedom of speech and movement. He was forbidden from speaking to more than one person at a time and couldn't attend his own son's birthday party. That same year, Mandela established the first Black law firm in South Africa with his old friend Tambo, and they represented African clients for free or at subsidized fees. Mandela thus fought the unjustness of the Apartheid not only on the political front but professionally as well. He faced racism at his job too as White witnesses refused to answer his questions in court. His ANC work, which pulled him away for long periods, started to take a toll on his career and family. He began losing parts of himself that made him who he was—a lawyer, a husband and a father—and arrived at his crossroads:

Path 1

Mandela could do it all. Of course time is limited, but it was his decision how to spend it and he wanted everything—a family, a career and an active political life. He had studied hard to open his practice to help people. And after drifting around for the past few years, it was good to come home to his wife and children. Was he being stretched thin? Yes, but surely there are moments of immense pressure in everyone's lives? It was just a phase he had to get through, and it would all be fine. It had to be.

Path 2

To mobilize and unite Africans for the cause, Mandela had to travel around the country. Doing so by buses and trains or hitchhiking added to his time away from the firm and his home. It hurt to hear his son ask him, in the rare occasions Mandela returned in time to tuck the boy in for the night, where Mandela had been and why he wasn't home more often. But thousands of other children were suffering in his country. As much joy leading a 'normal' family life would give him, the sad fact was that they led anything but normal lives—he and his people were treated like inferiors, as if their lives didn't matter. The struggle needed him and he could never deny that call.

Mandela separated from Mase in 1958, giving her the custody of their three children, while he fought against charges of treason. He married and had two daughters with Nomzamo Winifred Zanyiwe Madikizela (popularly known as Winnie Mandela). The majority of his second marriage was spent away from home, either hiding underground or in prison. While in prison, he lost his mother, and the following year his son Thembekile died in a car accident. Mandela was denied permission on both occasions to attend the funerals. He was allowed a letter twice a year, and most of them were either censored or burnt to torture the prisoners. For the longest time, he could only receive visitors every six months, and his daughters weren't permitted to see him in prison for the first 10 years. He spent 27 years in prison before he was released on 11 February 1990 to a country that had been waiting to see and hear from him for decades. Winnie and Mandela divorced in 1996, and their daughter Zindzi later spoke about how she had been deprived of her father and a childhood all her life and didn't see him much when he was working on the presidential campaign either. He served as the country's president from 1994 to 1999, and married for the third time on his eightieth birthday. For the next 15 years, he and his wife Graça Machel could finally experience the joys of a home and family in a free South Africa with their combined 45 grandchildren and great-grandchildren. On 5 December 2013, Mandela passed away at the age of 95.

LASTING LESSON

Human beings, at their core, can be insatiable. Undoubtedly we want it all: a well-paying job we love, a family in the various sizes and shapes it comes in, friends who care for us, hobbies we can devote ourselves to and free moments to kick off our shoes and relax. But we are beset by trickling time. Alas it—along with our resources, focus and energy— is limited and must be allocated according to our priorities. Mandela may have failed in performing the usual duties of a husband and father and forfeited his law career, but his decisions have to be weighed within his context. For him, politics came first, and his family knew that. While it is regrettable that they suffered as a consequence, no one could fault him for sacrificing aspects of his life for the sake of his country.

As much as we'd love to multitask and do everything, we will reach a point where that cannot be sustained. Either our bodies or minds will break down, or we would not be able to do justice to any of our projects because paying undivided attention on many fronts won't lead to success. As children we are usually encouraged to attempt everything in order to develop a well-rounded character, but as we grow older, our time becomes limited while our activities increase in depth and complexity. Then, making the tough choice to give preference to one endeavour over another becomes necessary (and is one of the lamentations of 'adulting'). We may have to forego pursuits we enjoy because there is something else that demands our attention. Perhaps our first priority is advancing in our chosen careers, and we may have to miss out on some fun vacations and parties. Or, we wish to focus on our family so may need to take a break from work. While we should always aim for balance, it may not always be possible. Rather than be disheartened at losing out on some things, we should instead think about the positive results that our concentrated energy can bring about. And the losses can be made easier to cope with once we realize the fundamental truth that:

SUCCESS REQUIRES SACRIFICE.

Nelson's Number

As the 466th prisoner at Robben Island in 1964, Nelson Mandela was given the prison number '46664'. He was identified by it throughout his time on Robben Island, but he later claimed it as his own in the fight against HIV/AIDS, to which he lost a son. Mandela gave the number to a global campaign that aimed at raising awareness about the epidemic. 46664 was established in 2002 as an independent not-for-profit organization. A series of concerts were organized to engage the youth of the world, the first of which took place in Cape Town where the likes of Beyoncé, Bono and Queen performed.

IT'S NEVER TOO LATE

Colonel Sanders (1890–1980)

Founder of KFC

*I think the moral of my life is don't quit at 65—maybe
your boat hasn't come in yet.*

Colonel Sanders

Fun fact—the smiling goateed man on the KFC bucket
isn't just a company mascot, unlike a certain red-haired
clown. Colonel Sanders was a living, breathing human
being responsible for the global spread of a classic southern
American dish: the fried chicken. While the restaurant came
from humble beginnings of operating out of a petrol station,
today the brand is worth $8.5 billion. With more than 20,000
outlets in over a 100 countries, it's not odd that *Forbes* counts
KFC among the top brands across all categories. Sanders
made the franchise model popular in the mid-twentieth
century and sold KFC in 1964 for $2 million. He stayed on
as the brand ambassador who personified 'southern gentility'
and even appeared on talk shows. The business rapidly grew
under aggressive marketing strategies and was sold again in
1971 for $285 million. The brand's value continued to rise,
and 15 years later, PepsiCo purchased it for almost triple that
amount. It is today operated by Yum! Brands, which also owns

Taco Bell and Pizza Hut.

The founding of Kentucky Fried Chicken sounds like the classic American success story, except that for most of his life, Sanders failed at all his professional ventures (and there were a *lot* of them). But he didn't abide by any narrative that told him he should've found success by so-and-so age. The end result was that he lived to see his creation steadily grow in national and international markets, until it became a household name.

BEFORE THE COLONEL

Harland David Sanders was born on 9 September 1890 on a farm in Indiana, United States, and was the eldest of three children. His father Wilbur, a butcher, unexpectedly died when Sanders was six. Sanders's mother Margaret Ann was thus forced to support the family by working at a cannery, peeling tomatoes. This left Sanders in charge of his brother and sister, and his duties included cooking their meals. A strict parent, their deeply religious mother taught the children to keep away from coffee, alcohol, tobacco, gambling and even whistling on Sundays, the Christian Lord's day.

When Sanders was 12, his mother married a man the children didn't get along with. Both sons consequently left home, with Sanders heading to a farm near Greenwood, Indiana. In exchange for the long hours spent toiling at the farm, he received a room and about $10 a month. He tried continuing his schooling alongside, but he got scared when the letters x and y entered his maths class in seventh grade and dropped out. Till age 15, he worked at the farm and then tried wearing several other hats—alas none truly fit.

He enlisted for the US army to fight in Cuba, but this wasn't how he earned the rank of a colonel. When it was discovered that Sanders was only 16, he was honourably discharged and sent back. He went to work for the railroad, a fascinating new operation that encapsulated the explorer's spirit in the beginning of the century. The scope of work was limited for him as he hadn't completed formal education. He began by scraping coal ash from steam engines. Keeping an observant eye on others, he gradually learnt the more skilled roles and progressed to them. Meanwhile, he overheard the risqué language that railroad workers used and absorbed swear words into his daily language (which would've probably shocked Mama Sanders). Reportedly, Sanders was obsessed with cleanliness and chose to wear white overalls yet returned home spotless after working around coal every day. However, his time at the railroad ended when he got into a fistfight with an engineer. Sanders's temper would become a refrain in his subsequent career-related failures.

At the age of 18, Sanders married Josephine King, and they had their first child within a year. They would go on to have two more, but unfortunately his only son died at the young age of 20. At a time when one didn't have to clear the bar exam to practise law in the Justice of the Peace Court, a 21-year-old Sanders began a law correspondence course. He did fulfil his wish in 1915, but that ended soon as well when he brawled with his own client in the courtroom. He then attempted operating his own ventures. One was a light company that supplied gas lamps, but it was doomed due to the advent of the electric bulb (a personality in this book can be blamed for that—Thomas Edison). Another was the establishment of a ferry service on an important crossing. It was profitable while it lasted, but it too died a quick death once a bridge was constructed on the spot. He also tried the role of a travelling Michelin tyre salesman though lost his job when he met with an accident, which he thankfully survived but his car did not. More can be added to the list: he sold insurance and once worked as a streetcar conductor, but like the other streams, these were short stints.

Sanders then set his gaze on the petrol station business, starting with managing a Standard Oil one in Nicholasville, Kentucky. This region faced two devastating events in the late 1920s—a drought that killed the crops and the Great Depression. These impacted the livelihoods of all people in the area. In 1930, Sanders shifted to Corbin, Kentucky, to manage a Shell Oil station. It was conveniently located at the fork of a busy highway. Here too, his hot-tempered streak carried on. He entered into an argument with the manager of a competitive petrol station over advertising space that ended with a gunfight in which Sanders's associate was shot and killed. Sanders shot the culprit in the shoulder, ending the debacle. Though Sanders was cleared of all charges, the other man was sentenced to 18 years in jail. From deaths to births, Sanders witnessed the full cycle of life in Corbin. Using his experience in helping birth his own three children, he worked as a midwife on the side, aiding women in communities that couldn't afford proper medical facilities. The services towards his community earned him the ceremonial state title of 'colonel' from the governor of Kentucky in the mid-1930s.

Corbin is where Sanders began experimenting with food as he started catering to weary travellers at his station. He hired waiting staff that served steak, ham, okra, string beans, potato dishes and biscuits (the savoury kind), but not fried chicken—

Sanders found the frying process too long to make it a feasible restaurant dish that met his high standards. In 1937, he added a motel to the station and eventually did away with the petrol station altogether. Along the way, he was introduced to the pressure cooker and adopted it in his kitchen experiments to shorten cooking times. It worked magic for vegetables, and he wondered if he could adapt it to frying chicken as well. This kicked off a long series of experiments with temperatures, oil types and ingredients until he perfected his secret recipe of southern fried chicken in 1940.

However, before much could be done with Sanders's new dish, the US entered World War II. At 52, Sanders was too old to serve, but he could offer his cooking and restaurant-managing skills at the secret city of Oak Ridge, Tennessee, one of the sites of the 'Manhattan Project'. The residents were hard at work on their own mysterious experiment of the atomic bomb that was used to eviscerate Hiroshima and Nagasaki in 1945. After the war, Sanders returned to his restaurant, which had expanded to accommodate nearly 150 customers. In 1947, Sanders and Josephine separated, and he married Claudia Ledington-Price two years later. Through these ups and downs in his personal life, his business venture—one that had finally been successful—faced its own hiccups. In the early fifties, the junction that had brought so much traffic to his restaurant was moved a bit further away, which impacted his business to some extent. Sanders then received news that a new freeway was to be built that would skip his town entirely. He saw what the future held—another failed business, that too in his mid-sixties—and stumbled upon his own crossroads:

Path 1

Genuinely, Sanders had thought he'd got it right this time around. That after repeated failures, he'd found something he was actually *good* at and, moreover, had enjoyed doing from his childhood. It should've worked! But the universe is cruel and always finds a way to get you down. And now, he was too old to do anything about it. All the people his age were retired and living on their savings, and Sanders had nothing, *nothing* to show for all his years of hard work. All he had was his restaurant, whose valuation had been slashed, and his social security checks—a measly $105 that came in every month. That's what retired senior citizens got, and he had to somehow make do with it.

Path 2

Sanders knew he had struck gold with his recipe, and the fault didn't lie with it or his behaviour this time around. Rather, it was an external circumstance that couldn't be helped. Sure, he had entered his sixties, but the fight hadn't left him. He really believed in his product and so did his customers—he had been recommissioned as a Kentucky colonel in honour of his cuisine in 1949. Everything was set up, ready for him to plunge at. All he had to do was work, which he never shied away from.

Aged 66, Colonel Sanders sold his restaurant for a loss and used that money to pay taxes and clear debts. He encashed his social security check and hit the road with cooking equipment in search of restaurants that could add his chicken and cracklin' gravy to their already-established menus, like a few had done in the early 1950s. To save money, he spent many nights sleeping in his car. He pitched to the restaurants by cooking his chicken for them in their kitchens, and if the staff responded positively, he cooked a few batches for their customers. He offered a service in which he sent premixed herbs and spices in order to retain the secrecy of his recipe and charged four cents (that later became five) for each full chicken the restaurant sold. In the process, he made his uniform an all-white suit with a black string tie and was never seen publicly in any other outfit. He used it to create his brand of the southern gentleman and bleached his goatee to keep it a consistent white too. It was all gruelling work, but it paid off. Word about his recipe spread through organic means, and within a couple of years, people travelled to meet *him* so that they could franchise his recipe. By 1960, 200 outlets offered the Colonel's chicken, and in three more years, that number tripled, earning him an annual profit of $300,000. Sanders sold the company in 1964, but remained the face of Kentucky Fried Chicken and worked well into his last years, even butting heads with the management on several occasions. He was diagnosed with leukaemia in 1980 and died at the age of 90 on 16 December that year.

LASTING LESSON

Every generation grows up with targets that they have to achieve by certain ages. For the present one, it goes along the lines of: finish school by 18 and then graduate from college by 21 or 22. Following that, either work for a few years or straight away pursue a Master's degree. Get married in mid- or late twenties, have kids—it goes on and on. Any deviation is frowned upon and creates immense stress for the person in question. Unlike machines though, humans don't come with a set of instructions. These rules become the norm in society, but they're not set in stone. Many need time to figure out what they want from life, what makes them tick, what they're good at. And we're all allowed to change our minds.

Imagine making a choice when we weren't fully aware of the situation we'd be getting into, then later realizing that what we had visualized was way off the mark. If we do not allow ourselves any leeway to skid off the designated path and try something else, we would all suffocate. Besides, age affects people differently—many enjoy good health in their so-called retirement years. No one should feel any compulsion to talk, act, dress in a certain way because of their age. There are so many of us who feel that our physical ages and the ages of our souls are at variance. If our health allows, why shouldn't we do things that bring us joy? For Sanders, it was work—he enjoyed it though he deemed it necessary to support himself and his family. It could also be a hobby. There might be optimum ages to pick up new skills, but that is not to say we can't learn new things once we're older. More importantly, we can *enjoy* them at any age. So, let's throw society's roadmap out of the window and decide for ourselves what we wish to do, whatever age we are, because:

IT'S NEVER TOO LATE.

Colonel's Curse

KFC became a traditional Christmas meal in Japan in the 1970s due to smart marketing campaigns. Outside each restaurant stood a life-sized statue of the Colonel, welcoming patrons. One such statue was chucked into the Dotonbori River by riotous celebrators when their baseball team won the 1985 Japan Championship. However, the team's luck gave out afterwards, and everyone attributed it to the 'Curse of the Colonel'—a punishment for desecrating his figurine. It was believed the team would never replicate its win until the statue was recovered and restored. Almost 25 years later, the statue was discovered and fished out of the river. It is incomplete though as it's missing its left hand and spectacles, and the team hasn't won again!

CHALLENGES REVEAL OUR BEST SELVES

Elon Musk (b. 1971)

Founder of SpaceX and Co-founder of Tesla

What we're hoping to do with SpaceX is to push the envelope and provide a reason for people to be excited and inspired to be human.

Elon Musk

The inspiration behind Robert Downey Jr's portrayal of Tony Stark in *Iron Man* is the twenty-first century's own tech genius, Elon Musk. An engineer, inventor, investor and serial entrepreneur, Musk consistently ventures into niche territories and defeats all odds. He has made a mark in the sectors of solar energy, electric vehicles and space exploration with SolarCity, Tesla and SpaceX, each a multibillion-dollar company. It is no surprise then that he's one of the wealthiest and most powerful people on earth. Musk's net worth is over $30 billion, but he hasn't reserved it all for himself. In 2012, he signed The Giving Pledge, in which he vowed to donate a majority of his wealth and has already begun with contributions to foundations dedicated to education, the environment and technological advancements, among others. As if being the CEO of two companies and chairman of a third wasn't enough, he chose to don other hats and founded organizations in the fields of artificial intelligence, neurotechnology and tunnel construction. In recognition of his work, he has been elected as a Fellow of The Royal Society and awarded medals by Fédération Aéronautique Internationale and the Royal Aeronautical Society.

Musk is revered today for bringing about innovations in varied spheres, but he was once the butt of the joke of exactly those industries and close to bankruptcy. His staunch belief in the significance of the work he was doing made him brave each obstacle and eventually forced the rest of the world to foster faith in his ideas too.

RISE OF THE ROCKET MAN

Elon Reeve Musk was born in Pretoria, South Africa, on 28 June 1971 as the oldest offspring of a South African father and Canadian-born mother. His father Errol was an engineer and mother Maye a model and nutritionist. They had two more children, a boy and a girl, but divorced in 1979.

Musk showed a leaning towards science from a young age. As a child, he overcame his fear of darkness by realizing it was silly to be scared of a lack of photons in the visible wavelength. He used to be so lost in his daydreams that he wouldn't respond to his name being called, which made his parents think he had hearing trouble. He was the youngest and shortest in class and didn't get along well with his peers. In fact, he was bullied and physically assaulted. As a result, he lessened social interaction and kept to his books. From comics to encyclopaedias, he loved reading anything he could lay his hands on. He bought his first computer at age 10 with money he had saved up. That same year, IBM conducted a test at his school and discovered that he had one of the highest aptitudes for computer programming they'd come across. They weren't wrong—he programmed his own space-themed computer game called Blastar around that time. Showing an entrepreneurial streak from their pre-teen years, Musk and his brother Kimbal planned on opening a gaming arcade near their school. They managed to get the lease for the space as well as the equipment, but their parents rejected the idea when their signature was required to gain a city permit. Musk ultimately sold the game code to a computer magazine for $500.

Till the 1990s, White South African men were forced to enter military service at age 17. While Musk was not against serving his country, he did not want to do so for a government that imposed Apartheid—this was before the African National Congress came into power with Nelson Mandela's presidential victory. Musk completed his schooling, applied for Canadian citizenship and left his birth country. Without much money, his only recourse was to stay with distant relatives in Canada. He was put to work on their farms, shovelling grain and tending vegetables, and later moved to Ontario to pursue a Bachelor's degree at Queen's University. This is where he met Justine Wilson, whom he would marry in 2000 and have a set of twins and triplets with, after sadly losing his firstborn son in infancy. Rarely attending class, he instead showed up for exams after reading the textbooks. He survived on a dollar a day during this time and earned some extra by helping a friend throw house parties at which attendees were charged a $5 CAD entry fee. After two years,

Musk transferred to the University of Pennsylvania in the United States on an academic scholarship to pursue a dual degree in economics and physics. He graduated in 1995 with a scholarship for a physics PhD at Stanford, but he dropped out after two days' attendance. He felt Stanford wasn't conducive to the kind of revolutionary work he wanted to do. Believing his time would be better utilized in the Internet boom, he made his way to Silicon Valley—the locus of the day's breakthroughs.

Musk asked his brother Kimbal to join him in Silicon Valley to start an Internet company, Zip2. It was a combination of the Yellow Pages and a mapping software to create the first online city listings. Between them, they had enough funds to either rent an office or a flat, and they chose the former, sleeping on sofas and showering at the local YMCA. In 1999, Compaq bought Zip2 for over $300 million, making Musk a 28-year-old millionaire with his personal take of $22 million. Still, he wasn't satisfied because the company hadn't made a great impact on the world, at least not in the way he wanted. While he had the option of retiring on an island somewhere, his focus was already on his next project, a sector that hadn't seen much innovation with the web—banking. Within a few months, he established X.com, a website that provided the conventional services of a bank with the added function of online transfers. It merged with its rivals in 2000 to become the now-famous PayPal. However, there remained a rift among the management and Musk was ousted from his role of the CEO. But by holding maximum shares in the company, he took home a whopping $180 million when eBay bought PayPal for $1.5 billion in 2002. The makers of PayPal went on to create fantastic ventures of their own, including YouTube and LinkedIn, and Musk was no exception.

This time around, Musk could've purchased a *chain* of islands with his PayPal buyout, but his eyes were aimed high at the sky. Growing up in the seventies, the excitement of the Apollo 11 moon landing pervaded his life. Like many others, he expected humans to reach Mars within a few decades, except that human-led space missions declined in their reach over the years. In order to recreate the exhilaration from his childhood, Musk founded and became the CEO of SpaceX, or Space Exploration Technologies, in 2002, with a philanthropic aim. The original plan was to land a greenhouse on Mars, a photo of which—lush greenery against the red planet— would revitalize interest in approaching the planet again, with the ultimate goal of settling a colony on Mars to make humans a multi-planetary species. But he soon realized that even if he did create the *will*, it would be of no use without the *way*, as the costs of space missions had only increased over the decades. He found that Russian space missions were cheaper than NASA's, but their price quotations for rockets were almost double his budget too. Moreover, there was a marked difference between the cost of raw materials and the finished product, so he approached the problem differently. He considered innovating the process of rocket construction to lower expenses. Along with that, he began exploring reusable rockets, since the majority of the cost pertained to the parts that were discarded in flight. Alas, he was ridiculed for his ideas, and many saw him as an immigrant, with no relevant qualifications, attempting to commercialize space exploration and stand up to powerful government agencies. That didn't deter Musk. Although he was *literally* learning rocket science, he pored over books and brought along talented engineers from top organizations. Musk had funded the company almost entirely himself and budgeted for three launches—all of which unfortunately failed.

In 2004, Musk invested close to $6.5 million in the electric-car company Tesla Motors and joined its board of directors as the chairman. At the time, huge SUVs such as the Hummer were in fashion and, again, industry experts called Musk an outsider who didn't know what he was doing. Tesla not only wanted to create electric vehicles that were better for the environment, but also make them alluring to petrol-car owners as viable replacements. The company's plan was to first roll out a premium high-performance sports car at low volumes to show that electric cars could be thrilling and beautiful, then a mid-range family sedan in medium volumes and finally low-priced cars in high volumes. But design and production costs of the sports car skyrocketed and required further investments from Musk's PayPal fund.

Along with sustainable energy consumption, Musk ventured into sustainable energy creation. He invested in SolarCity in 2006, a start-up that provided the assembly and maintenance of solar panels. For all three enterprises, Musk had originally set aside half of his PayPal earnings, about $90 million, but over time realized he had been too optimistic and would need to increase his investments. Whereas SolarCity was performing all right, Tesla and SpaceX were in trouble. Musk had somehow scraped together enough funding for a fourth SpaceX rocket launch, which was finally a success in 2008. He also took over as CEO of Tesla, which released its first car, the Roadster, that same year, after many delays. The year was looking up, but then the market crashed while company funds in the bank depleted. On the personal front, his life wasn't faring any better—he separated from his wife that year as well. These elements combined made 2008 the worst year in Musk's life, and he came across a crossroads:

Path 1

Everything was going wrong. His marriage fell apart. And why did he have to enter such untested, high-risk fields at work? People had told him he was making a mistake—one of his friends had even shown him videos of rockets exploding when Musk was about to begin work on SpaceX. He should now cut his losses and look for safe bets he could back. Perhaps, if he was lucky, one day he could recover his PayPal fortune.

Path 2

Would that satisfy him though? The jackpot Musk had hit with the sale of Zip2 was unprecedented, but it didn't make him feel like he had done something worthwhile that could alter the world. And that's what he believed his purpose was—to help create change for the better. It sounded daunting, but it thrilled him. The prospect of charting new territories gave him the motivation to wake every morning and be happy about going to work. He couldn't let the investments he had made in Tesla and SpaceX amount to nothing, even if it meant he had to pour in all of his remaining capital.

Musk put in his leftover fortune into Tesla and SpaceX to save them. He had completely exhausted his own funds and had to borrow money from friends to pay rent. Three months after SpaceX's successful flight that substantiated his talks, the company received a $1.6 billion contract from NASA to resupply the International Space Station. The news couldn't have come at a better time since the company was days away from sinking. For the longest period, Musk hadn't sought outside investment in his companies because he felt that if *he* wasn't willing to back his work with his own capital, neither should others. Gradually, the industry began noticing the advancements that both companies brought about and his ventures received external investments and contracts. Today they generate billions of dollars' worth of revenue. Tesla bought SolarCity in 2016 and has launched more cars, while SpaceX has proved that rockets can be reused with the successful return and landing of the first stage of the Falcon 9 rocket and its usage in subsequent flights. Many other companies have followed the path Musk painstakingly dug, with electric cars being released by big names such as BMW, Audi and Jaguar. New commercial space exploration organizations have also arisen, such as United Launch Alliance, a collaboration between Boeing and Lockheed Martin.

LASTING LESSON

Two facets define us—nature and nurture. Who we are at our core versus what society and our circumstances make us. Because we operate within set rules, the expectations that society has from us and those we have from ourselves are replicated within our communities. Yet, there is something to be said of unique thoughts and ideas. As Musk explains it, there are two ways of approaching things: reasoning by analogy or taking the physics route. The first comes in handy—and is necessary in fact—when we're doing daily tasks, such as walking or writing. We use the ways that already exist, making slight variations to fit our circumstances. But what happens when we attempt something entirely new? The existing methods won't prove useful as a frame of reference then. Physics contains laws that are fundamental truths, but we have only reached them by questioning everything, even if the questions went against what we considered common sense. Due to this, rarely do people venture into uncharted territories. Though when they do, they change the world forever, like the brains behind the wheel and the typewriter did. However, change begins from within. Before we can confront the truisms of the outside world, we have to question what *we* think and what we believe our abilities and capabilities are because:

CHALLENGES REVEAL OUR BEST SELVES.

Musk and Mars

Musk's vision for SpaceX is to send colony settlements to the red planet in order to make the human race a multi-planetary species and also have another civilization in place in case disasters like climate change or another world war destroy the earth. He hopes the colony on Mars can be achieved within his lifetime. In fact, he wishes to die on Mars. In the pursuit of reaching the planet, SpaceX launched a test flight of Falcon Heavy in 2018. Instead of using concrete blocks for the dummy payload, as is the norm, Musk sent his old cherry-red Tesla Roadster with a mannequin in an astronaut suit called 'Starman'. The car and mannequin are still out in space and will likely tour it for millions of years.

FOCUS ON THE BIG PICTURE

Serena Williams (b. 1981)

Tennis player

I set my goal for just what was in sight, and I think subconsciously, a lot of people set their goal on what's already there. Why not reach for a higher goal?

Serena Williams

Serena Williams has changed the way women's tennis is played and perceived. Originally introduced to us as one-half of the Williams sisters duo, Serena Williams has etched a mark not just in doubles tournaments played alongside her elder sister Venus, but as an exceptional talent in her own right. She has spent over 300 weeks as the top player in Women's Tennis Association (WTA) rankings, won the Olympic gold and currently holds the record for the most Grand Slam singles wins in the Open Era—23 as opposed to the men's record holder, Roger Federer, who has collected 20. She claimed her last Grand Slam title, the 2017 Australian Open, while she was *eight weeks pregnant*. She is the highest-paid female athlete in the world due to her endorsements and prize winnings. She has a net worth of $225 million, making her the only athlete on *Forbes* magazine's list of America's Richest Self-Made Women. Williams has also expanded her portfolio to include the roles of fashion designer, actor, author, philanthropist and investor. Not only has she, along with her sister, been credited with ushering in an age of power and athleticism in women's tennis, she has used her voice to bring attention to racial and gender discrimination in sports.

Williams comes from modest roots and faced many hardships in life, but she has been unstoppable since she bagged her first major title at age 17. Despite this string of successes, she momentarily lost sight of her ultimate goal and became her own worst enemy, but a change in her mindset helped her break several sports records and be hailed as the champion of tennis.

THE WOMAN, THE CHAMPION

Born in Michigan, United States, to Richard Williams and Oracene Price on 26 September 1981, Serena Jameka Williams grew up as the youngest of five girls, three of whom are her half-sisters. Even before the Williams duo was born, Richard had decided to steer them towards tennis and had a huge impact on their lives through his unconventional parenting. In 1978, Richard caught a bit of the French Open on TV and was astounded when the winner was presented with a cheque of $40,000, whereas he earned about that much in a year. Determined to give his family a better life, he pushed his children towards the sport. The older ones didn't take to it, but the youngest two showed promise. Richard wasn't a tennis player himself but decided to learn more about it through instructional videos and tennis magazines and wrote a 78-page plan outlining his daughters' professional tennis careers. They were homeschooled by their mother while their father coached them on the court for up to six hours a day. Williams was about four when she first entered the tennis court. Around that time, the family moved to the Compton area of California, notorious for its gang violence. A far cry from what professional athletes are used to, the girls practised at the cracked and littered public tennis courts with gunshots echoing in the backdrop. The move to Compton was deliberate on Richard's part as he believed that growing up in a rough neighbourhood would toughen his children for any obstacles they would face later in life.

In the nineties, younger players usually entered the junior circuit first before making a name for themselves in the major titles, but Richard wanted to keep his girls away from the pressures of that life for as long as possible. In 1991, the family moved to Florida so that the two could be coached by Rick Macci at his prestigious tennis academy. A few days after their arrival, the sisters began an intense fitness regimen that involved taekwondo, boxing, gymnastics and ballet. Their game improved, and word spread about their talent though they weren't competing in junior tournaments. The sisters enrolled in Driftwood Academy, a private school in Florida, in 1995. The same year, Richard took over as their trainer and coach, a move that forced everyone to raise a sceptical brow.

Williams made her WTA debut in 1997 and cracked the top 350 WTA ranking later that year. Her performance on the court spelt great things to come, and she received a juicy five-year $12 million deal from Puma even before she had graduated from high school. The following year, she nabbed her first WTA doubles titles with her sister and entered the top 20 ranking. In June 1998, she made her debut at Wimbledon but had to forfeit the singles tournament because of a knee injury, although she won the mixed doubles final and thus her first Grand Slam title. She replicated this win at the US Open. In 1999, the duo became the first sister act to win a Grand Slam doubles title at the French Open at ages 17 and 18. Two months later, Williams won her first singles Grand Slam at the US Open, making history by being the first African-American woman to win a Grand Slam in the Open Era. The US Open was the title she had been vying for since she was a child, while Venus had her eyes set on the French Open, which was coincidentally her first Grand Slam singles win.

From this point onwards, there was no holding back Williams as she claimed title after title. She also ventured into acting by grabbing spots in TV shows such as *My Wife and Kids* and *Street Time* in the early 2000s and many more since then. Holding a keen interest in fashion, she launched her own label, Aneres, which is her name spelt backwards. But she hasn't been a stranger to controversies. Having proved herself a better player than her sister in face-offs, rumours of match-fixing floated around when Venus finally did beat Serena in the Wimbledon semi-finals of 2000. There were also whispers surrounding their father, painting him as the puppeteer pulling the strings behind the scenes. Yet, the sisters kept their cool when the journalists' focus shifted from their games to malicious allegations against their father, and the two always shrugged off the negative comments. The family has faced tough times together as well, with the divorce of Richard and Oracene in 2002 and the death of Williams's oldest half-sister, Yetunde Price, in a 2003 shooting in Compton, not far from where the sisters used to play tennis. Williams also faced medical issues, including a pulmonary embolism in 2011 that could've ended her career, and even her life, had she not got surgeries in time.

Williams recovered from her health scares and braved family tragedies to continue triumphing on the court. By 2014, she had won 17 Grand Slam single tournaments. She felt the pressure of getting the eighteenth so she could tie with legendary tennis players Chris Evert and Martina Navratilova, and have her name counted among the top five female tennis players of all time. But something was wrong. Despite being number one, the eighteenth win kept slipping through her fingers as she lost one title after another, bringing her face to face with her crossroads:

Path 1

The pressure was on. Not just from the fans, other athletes and the media, but from within. Williams was rank one, and she had to maintain it. More importantly, the goal of matching the icons who had come before her was within grasp, and she *had* to get to 18 wins. She could hear it all the time: *18, 18, 18!* This was the year she did it—she could feel it in her bones—and there would be no stopping her eighteenth victory.

Path 2

But why *just* 18? It was not like Williams was going to retire after the next win. Why restrict herself to a particular number merely because it was a significant point in someone else's journey? She needed to think of her own path, which wasn't coming to a dead-end anytime soon. She had to change her mindset to think of the big picture, of what she eventually wanted, and not concentrate solely on her next target. Her journey was that of a marathon runner, and she would not be satisfied with only a single milestone.

Serena Williams had an epiphany after a talk with her coach, who asked her why she was beating herself up for a number that was in no way emblematic of her career. He told her that she should instead think of higher goals, like that of 30 or 40 major wins. This simple exchange shifted her perspective and made her consider the unexplored possibilities of her tennis career. It released the pressure that had been building inside her, and she won the next Grand Slam she participated in, the US Open. She went on to claim the three subsequent Grand Slams as well, thus marking her second 'Serena Slam', where she was the reigning champion of all four Grand Slams simultaneously (her first was in 2002–2003).

In 2017, Williams married Alexis Ohanian, the famous co-founder of Reddit, and had her first child with him. She currently holds 23 Grand Slam titles and has no intention of backing down. She even used her celebrity to question the unfairness female athletes had to face regarding a drop in their WTA rankings when they took a break from the game due to pregnancy, and she challenged the stereotype of tennis as a White person's 'country club sport' to make it more approachable to people from all races, genders and classes.

LASTING LESSON

Focusing on the end goal or setting higher goals may at first seem counterintuitive. Wouldn't the looming grand objective increase our stress instead of easing it? But being fixated on a single component can make us short-sighted and trip us over. Reminding ourselves of the end game encourages us to gradually take one step after another until we reach our final destination. In fact, if we set our aim low, we may never realize our full potential. If we go by the standards that have been traditionally set, we probably won't push ourselves to explore other methods and avenues and will create restrictions before we've discovered all the possibilities. And when we do accomplish that lower aim, we may be at a loss of what to do next. The fire to keep working, learning and improving to achieve our final objective is what sustains us. More importantly, having our ultimate aim in mind also helps us multitask and work smarter. Consider the case of a student overburdened by course load during exam time. They may want to be perfectionists and learn every single thing, but it may not be humanly possible under time constraints. Instead of obsessing over every chapter, they could take a look at the weightage of each and study in a smarter way to ensure that they're able to score what they had wanted *overall*. Thus, we can not only relieve the pressure we suffer through for tasks that may be insignificant in the grand scheme of things, we can expand our limits if we remember to:

FOCUS ON THE BIG PICTURE.

Serena's Strength

Richard Williams is famous (and at times infamous) for his unorthodox parenting and coaching methods. Reportedly, during one of the Williams sisters' practice sessions in Compton, he had them surrounded by children their age who hurled insults at the girls, just so they could learn to focus on their game through anything. This may seem heartless, but it turned out to be prophetic in a way when Serena Williams was booed during the finals at the Indian Wells tournament in 2001. The crowd even cheered (more accurately, jeered) when she committed a double fault. The spectators reacted so because of the rumours of match-fixing, but Richard stated that it was racially motivated, since people in the crowd had called him racial expletives. Williams retained her cool and won the match but boycotted the tournament for 13 years.

HARNESS EVERY TEAMMATE'S STRENGTH

Walt Disney (1901–1966)

Co-founder of The Walt Disney Company

Of all the things I've done, the most vital is coordinating those who work with me and aiming their efforts at a certain goal.

Walt Disney

hildhoods of many generations would have been incomplete without the creations of Walt Disney. Long after his death, we continue to be surrounded by his legacy. Whether we watch The Walt Disney Company films, buy its character figurines from toy shops or visit one of the famous amusement parks, there is no escape from the brand. And if someone thinks they've managed to remain immune because the company's films are aimed at children, they would be sorely mistaken. With the acquisition of Marvel Entertainment in 2009, Lucasfilm in 2012 and 20th Century Fox in 2019, even fans of Marvel comics, films and TV shows as well as *Star Wars*, *Deadpool*, *Die Hard*, *Titanic* and *Fight Club* are all technically now consuming products touched by The Walt Disney Company. The amassed success has led to the company having an estimated net worth of $130 billion, with accolades to match. Along with his staff, Walt Disney received upwards of 950 global honours and citations. In fact, he holds the record for the maximum Academy Award wins. Some of his other laurels include the Presidential Medal of Freedom, Thailand's Order of the Crown, Brazil's Order of the Southern Cross and Showman of the World Award from the National Association of Theatre Owners. What's more, a minor planet discovered in 1980 was also named in his honour—4017 Disneya.

However, even one of the most successful people to have ever lived had to try multiple times to establish a profitable venture and was in one instance also forced to file for bankruptcy. While Disney altered tactics through all his failed attempts, his most significant change lay in the way he built teams and interacted with them.

THE MAN BEHIND THE BRAND

Walter Elias Disney was born in Chicago, United States, on 5 December 1901 to Elias and Flora Disney, and was the fourth of five children. When Disney was four, the family moved to a small farm in Marceline, Missouri. He started school late, around the age of eight, and thus had a lot of time growing up to explore different interests. He first received encouragement from neighbours to create art—he drew one such neighbour's horse in exchange for a nickel. The family spent a happy, if at times financially tough, four years in Marceline until a bad case of typhoid and pneumonia left Elias weakened and unfit for farm work. They then moved to the bigger Kansas City in 1911.

Gone were Disney's leisurely days as he, along with his

elder brother Roy, had to wake up every day at 4:30 a.m. to deliver papers on a newspaper route Elias had purchased. They made one round before school and another in the evenings, at times to grand houses on whose lawns Disney would pause to admire discarded fancy toys. Kansas City was also the place where he first showed interest in entertainment. Inspired by Charlie Chaplin, Disney performed vaudeville acts with a friend.

Disney wasn't interested in school, and the paper route and other odd jobs took their toll on his studies anyway. In one of his summer breaks, he followed his brother into the 'news butcher' business in which he sold newspapers, sweets and soft drinks to passengers on trains. To land the role, he lied about being 16, a birthday that was still a couple of months away. However, he was careless with his stock and ended up being in debt to his employer. Big brother Roy had to swoop in to settle Disney's losses, which would perhaps set a precedent for later years. The family moved back to Chicago in 1917, where Disney attended high school. He continued working, first at a jelly factory and later at the post office, for which he fibbed about his age once again (and not for the last time). He took night art classes thrice a week at The Chicago Academy of Fine Arts, which was the sole formal training he received as an artist apart from some classes he had taken as a child in Kansas City. Not shy about sharing his art, he published his cartoons in the school's newspaper.

Roy entered the navy soon after the US joined its allies in World War I. Taking a cue from his brother again, Disney wished to join the war effort as well, but he was too young to do so in 1918. He heard of a Red Cross unit that would accept 17-year-olds and *once more* falsified his age, thus ending his formal education at eighth standard. By the time he arrived in France, Germany had signed the armistice. Still, he stayed back a year to help with post-war operations. He continued drawing on the side and submitted them to humour magazines albeit only to receive rejections. When he returned to the US in 1919, he wanted to avoid the sort of physically demanding work he had grown up doing. Plus, he knew what he wanted to be—an artist.

Disney joined a commercial art studio in Kansas City. The drawing board engrossed him to the extent that he avoided toilet breaks as much as he could. He had a colleague named Ub Iwerks. After being laid off from the studio due to cost-cutting measures, they began their own enterprise in 1920. Iwerks–Disney Commercial Artists, funded by Disney's savings, lived a short life. Though their first month's earnings weren't bad for a fledgling company, Disney received a much better offer somewhere else. After discussing it with Iwerks, Disney left their start-up to join the role of an animator at an ad company, and Iwerks followed suit. Mostly self-taught, Disney learnt about animation from library books that addressed the rising popularity of the medium. He incorporated these learnings and his own ideas into his work, which was appreciated by some but not all: his immediate superior thought him 'too inquisitive'. Disney somehow convinced his boss to lend him a camera so that he could experiment at home. It resulted in a cartoon Disney titled 'Laugh-O-gram', which he sold to Newman Theatre. Tongue-tied when asked for the price of each reel, he blurted the amount it cost him to make. Although he landed a customer from whom he earned no profit, he was happy to be doing something he loved. Disney soon learnt how laborious the work was for one person, especially since he was still working at his day job at the ad company, so he built a team at Laugh-O-gram Films, which he gave his full attention to from 1922. Iwerks also joined him that year. Still learning the tricks of animation himself, Disney guided his team of even lesser experienced folk through the first few projects while they rapidly ate through their capital. Though he signed a contract with a distributor, Disney agreed to the strange conditions of receiving $100 as down payment with a balance of $11,000 not due for another one-and-a-half years, which would've been fine had the company any capital, but that wasn't the case! By the end of the year, employees stopped being paid and the company survived due to small loans from well-wishers and local businessmen. Living in the studio space and eating in limited quantities, Disney himself scraped by thanks to Roy's generosity.

In 1923, Disney took on his hardest project yet and combined animation with live-action in *Alice's Wonderland*. But, before the public could lay their eyes on it, Laugh-O-gram Films went bankrupt. Leaving that chapter behind, he moved to Hollywood. He'd hang around studio lots, trying to pick up tricks of the trade. Here, he struck up a deal with cartoon distributor Margaret Winkler by sending her a sample of *Alice's Wonderland*. This was the beginning of a great new partnership for Disney, or so he believed at the time.

Disney recruited his brother Roy to help him with the business side of running the company though he continued to take most decisions. And that's how the Disney Brothers Studio was formed, which later became Walt Disney Productions. Their team grew and was busy with projects, but the brothers sometimes delayed their own salaries because of cash-flow problems. In 1924, Disney hired Iwerks, and the following year, Disney married an ink artist at the company, Lillian Bounds, with whom he would have a daughter and adopt another girl. Bit by bit, Winkler's husband Charles Mintz took over the dealings, but he shared a strained relationship with Disney. Mintz asked for new material to distribute through Universal, one of Hollywood's major studios. Wishing to delve into full animation, Disney and his team created the character Oswald the Lucky Rabbit, which became a huge hit.

The contract for the Oswald character was up for renewal with the Winklers in 1928. Hoping to renegotiate terms, Disney instead found himself in a series of shocking meetings where he learnt that Mintz expected Disney to surrender his role as an independent businessman. The final nail in the coffin was hammered when Oswald was taken away from him, as negotiations fell through because Universal owned the rights to the character. Although Disney's train ride back home led him in one direction, there lay a crossroads in front of him that would determine the rest of his life:

Path 1

After the failures of Iwerks–Disney Commercial Artists and Laugh-O-gram Films, Disney thought he had finally created a successful business, only to have everything of worth stolen from him. Surely, this was a sign for him to give up? Most who came to Hollywood struggled and never achieved their goals, and perhaps he was among those unlucky ones. He had a beautiful wife who loved him, and he needed to support her and the children he would have one day. He should cast his big-city dreams aside and go for a more conventional job, like his father and other relatives, since he clearly couldn't do this by himself.

Path 2

Yes, Disney couldn't do this by himself, not everything. While he wasn't the most talented of artists or a smooth businessman, what he was good at was cooking up creative ideas. So, he sat and concentrated, and he saw it—a mouse! He would create a new character, a mouse. He'd call him Mortimer Mouse... no, that sounded too stuffy. What about 'Mickey'? He went straight to Iwerks with the complicated sketch he'd made, and Iwerks refined it to make Mickey easier to animate. And that's how the pair created the iconic character that would be recognized as the logo of the entertainment behemoth, The Walt Disney Company.

The first two Mickey Mouse cartoons weren't picked up by distributors, but then Disney had the idea of adding sound and perfectly synchronizing it with the action—a rare treat for animations at the time—and they gradually took off. Next, he set his eyes on creating feature-length animated films, starting with *Snow White and the Seven Dwarfs*, which was dubbed 'Disney's folly' because industry experts believed no one would want to sit through it. Instead, Disney was presented with an honorary Oscar award for the film, which included one usual statue and seven mini statuettes depicting the seven dwarfs! Disney followed this with the successful *Fantasia*, *Pinocchio* and the live-action *Mary Poppins*. As the company grew, he began concentrating on what he did best—leading the creative direction. He had long stopped doing the animation himself but guided his staff on story development. He wasn't a great artist, so he created a skilled team that could carry out his vision. All his teams were full of talented people, so much so that members from his original team went on to create their own popular brands and characters, such as Bugs Bunny, Daffy Duck and Tweety Bird. He had the uncanny ability of recognizing hidden talents in others and bringing them to the fore. He set Xavier Atencio, a man who had exclusively done storyboarding for animation, to work on a script for a pirate ride in one of Disney's amusement parks because he saw Xavier's potential. Disney didn't let petty squabbles hinder his way either—to direct his biggest American live-action project, *20,000 Leagues Under the Sea*, Disney chose Richard Fleischer, the son of an early competitor. Fleischer hadn't done any big projects, but Disney had a gut feeling that proved true. His early decision to get his brother on board to handle the business aspect of the company likewise had rewarding results. Roy Disney is still thought to be one of entertainment history's greatest corporate leaders and Walt Disney a master storyteller—he was a natural actor, even providing the voice for Mickey Mouse for many years, and had a great sense of comedy and drama. Having been a heavy smoker from his time in France, he died 10 days after his sixty-fifth birthday, on 15 December 1966, due to lung cancer.

LASTING LESSON

Self-reliance is a brilliant ideal to aspire to, but often great projects are exclusively achieved through fruitful collaborations, that is, teamwork in which each individual brings along their best skills and fills each other's gaps. As much as we'd like to be perfect, it is a sad truth that we can never attain that state. A successful team leader must recognize their own strengths and weaknesses and those of the people around them and focus on getting everybody to shine their brightest. This lesson of course not only applies in the corporate sphere, but also in team sports and group projects. Take the case of the latter—one may be great at creating presentations, while another may be skilled at research, the third at content and so on. It would be wise to delegate in such a manner that everyone can focus on a task they excel at. The end result of the teamwork would be a combination of everybody's expertise. Not only would it capitalize on each person's skillset, but it would make the assignment enjoyable as well since we usually like doing activities we're good at. By the end, we would have a product in which every team member has fully utilized their talents, and we would incorporate their passion during the process, which always tips things over the edge. And all this can be achieved if we remember to:

HARNESS EVERY TEAMMATE'S STRENGTH.

Disney and the Dame

Before starring in the classics *The Sound of Music* and *Mary Poppins*, Dame Julie Andrews acted on stage. After a performance in 1962, Walt Disney approached Andrews backstage and asked her if she would like to fly to Los Angeles to see what he had been prepping for his first-ever live action film, *Mary Poppins*. She was excited at the opportunity but couldn't leave as she was four months pregnant. He told her he would wait for her to return to work and even asked her then-husband Tony Walton, who was just starting out as a costume and set designer in the London scene, to bring his portfolio. Disney saw something special in the couple, and he was right. Andrews got the lead in the movie, which launched her career in Hollywood and earned her an Oscar, and Walton received an Oscar nomination for his work on the film's set and costumes.

CHOOSE INSPIRATION OVER COMPARISON

Albert Einstein (1879–1955)

Physicist

Valuable achievement can sprout from human society only when it is sufficiently loosened to make possible the free development of an individual's abilities.

Albert Einstein

It's safe to say that someone has been immortalized for their intellect when their name becomes synonymous with the word 'genius', as is the case for the entry 'Einstein' in dictionaries. Dr Albert Einstein's physical appearance also gave birth to a new caricature of the 'mad scientist' in popular culture, with wild outgrown grey hair and dishevelled clothing. Hailed as the successor of Isaac Newton, Einstein challenged the basic foundations of science because he perceived the world in ways no one else could. In 1905, dubbed as his 'miracle year', he wrote five scientific papers. One of these won him the 1921 Nobel Prize in Physics, another earned him his doctorate and a third put forth the world's most famous equation, $E = mc^2$. He published more than 300 papers in his lifetime, his focus ranging from the microscopic photons to the massive cosmos. His theories live on in the technology we use today: lasers, fibre optics, nuclear power and even space travel. Eventually, he won most awards and honours that the scientific world has to offer—he was elected to the Royal Society, awarded the Gold Medal of the Royal Astronomical Society and conferred with honorary degrees from several universities, including but not limited to Oxford, Cambridge, Harvard and Princeton. It's easy to see why he is referred to as the most influential physicist of the twentieth century.

Having published his five revolutionary papers at the tender age of 26, one would assume that Einstein achieved success quite easily in life. But struggle does not discriminate— even geniuses aren't immune to hardship and failure.

THE MAN BEHIND THE GENIUS

On 14 March 1879, Albert Einstein was born to a Jewish family at Ulm in Württemberg, Germany. He was the firstborn of Pauline and Hermann Einstein, a high-school graduate turned businessman. The couple also had a girl two years later. Einstein didn't speak till age two, and afterwards, he would first whisper the words to himself and only then say them aloud to the person he wished to address. His parents consulted a doctor regarding it as they were concerned over this 'abnormal' behaviour, while adults referred to the toddler as 'dopey' and 'almost backwards'.

The family relocated to Munich a year after Einstein's birth, where he attended a Catholic school as his parents were irreligious. As the lone Jew in class, Einstein didn't face any discrimination from teachers, but his fellow students were another story. Ethnically motivated physical and verbal attacks from other children instilled in him the sense of being an outsider. At age nine, he went to the Luitpold Gymnasium high school, where he encountered a strict educational system that he felt thwarted his creativity and individuality. A teacher went as far as telling Einstein that he would never amount to anything (no points for guessing if that teacher eventually regretted their words or not). While we may scoff at that insult now thanks to the gift of hindsight, imagine being a child and hearing an authority figure proclaim that your future was doomed.

From a young age, Einstein was curious about the workings of the universe. The first time he came across a compass, he was fascinated by the phenomenon of invisible forces deflecting the needle. He made the quest of learning more about unseen forces a passion that lasted a lifetime. He was also a visual thinker and rarely thought in words. In fact, thoughts first entered his mind in images, and he later tried to express them using words. For fun, he ignored the company of kids in favour of creating his own proofs of mathematical theorems. His mother, an accomplished pianist, passed down her love of music to her son. She fixed violin lessons for him, which he initially despised. But he slowly fell in love with music and would later use it to help himself think whenever he was beset by problems. A family friend, Max Talmud, informally tutored the teenage Einstein on higher mathematics and philosophy. Talmud gave Einstein *Critique of Pure Reason* by the philosopher Immanuel Kant and was astonished to find that the book that seemed so opaque to adults was grasped by the young Einstein.

In 1894, Einstein was left with distant relatives in Germany so that he could complete his education while his family moved to Italy due to misfortunes regarding his father's work. As a sceptic and rebel, Einstein questioned everything, even the authority of his elders. This trait didn't endear him to teachers, and he detested his time at school. He managed to stick it out for a few months but finally ran away to his parents' house. A major impetus for leaving Germany was the military duty he would have been forced to join upon turning 17, which, as a pacifist, he didn't agree with. Nonetheless, what his parents opened their door to was a school dropout and army draft dodger, with a promising future nowhere in sight. Some hope remained as he could gain admission to the Federal Polytechnic School in Zurich, Switzerland, without a high school diploma if he passed its tough entrance examinations. Although he was two years too young to meet the age requirement, a family friend wrote to the school, asking it to make an exception for the child prodigy. The school granted Einstein permission to sit the exams, albeit with a dose of doubt. While he prepped, he wrote his first paper on theoretical physics at age 16. In 1895, he appeared for the exams and scored high in mathematics and physics but didn't fare well in other subjects. He didn't gain admission, but a professor suggested that Einstein audit some classes. He chose to finish formal schooling instead.

To this effect, Einstein joined a special high school in Aarau, Switzerland, that encouraged visual thinking and individuality—a perfect match for Einstein who had rebelled against rote learning. It was at this school that he began his thought experiment of what it would be like to ride alongside a beam of light, matching its speed, which he pondered for the next 10 years. In 1896, Einstein graduated from the school and renounced his German citizenship, scorning the country's growing militarist atmosphere. Although he finally gained admission to the Polytechnic for a four-year mathematics and physics teaching diploma, he wasn't looked upon favourably by the staff. He often didn't show up for class because he studied advanced subjects on his own, and the teachers felt disrespected in return. When he did attend class, he preferred following his own methods of experimentation and candidly questioned his professors why they didn't teach the advancements being made. Without their support, he unfortunately failed to find any teaching position after graduating in 1900. In fact, he was the only one from his section who wasn't offered a post at the Polytechnic. This was made even tougher because his application for a Swiss citizenship was granted on the condition that he must work in a permanent job. At one point, he even thought of switching fields and entering the insurance business, a step he thankfully didn't take.

At the Polytechnic, Einstein had begun a relationship with the sole woman in the mathematics and science section, Mileva Marić. His family opposed the match because they objected to her Serbian background and their age difference—she was four years older—but that did not hinder the couple. They had a child outside of marriage in 1902, a little girl named Lieserl, but little is known of her (it is believed that she was given up for adoption and either lived on till the 1990s or died of scarlet fever as a child). Einstein felt he couldn't support a family without a job. Desperate, he began tutoring children but did not last long in these assignments. His fortune seemed to turn around when a connection recommended him for the role of a third-class patent examiner at the Swiss Patent Office in Bern. The happy spell didn't endure, because alongside this news came terrible tidings that his father had been taken ill. Hermann Einstein died in October 1902. On his deathbed, he finally gave his son the blessing to marry Marić. Einstein regretted that his father died thinking his son a failure. The disappointment that he believed to have been in his father's eyes must have threatened to open the floodgates of all the negativity that had accumulated in his life, and he found himself at a crossroads with two distinct routes:

Path 1

As the only graduate from his class who couldn't find a teaching spot, Einstein had to resort to working in a clerical position. Why couldn't he be more like his peers? He had even published a paper for the first time in 1901, but it had received no response from the scientific community. He'd also submitted an attempt at a doctoral dissertation that year, but it had been rejected. Who could really blame him if he gave up on his passion for physics? At least he had a job now, as inglorious as it may be. He needed to go to the office, work and try to catch up to his peers who had all left him behind in the Snakes and Ladders game that life can be. Who knows, perhaps one day he could become the head of the Swiss Patent Office?

Path 2

It's true that Einstein had always been different. He asked too many questions, his interests were alternative and he didn't have any reverence for religion or authority. He began speaking at a later age as well, but he picked up concepts in his favourite subjects much quicker than everybody else. What was there to gain from comparing his growth with others' then? He finally had a steady income, so he could marry and support Marić, but the naysayers shouldn't dissuade him from following his passion. As always, he would do things his way, in his own time, and hope for the best.

Einstein was all in, although he couldn't have known that the desk job would turn out to be a blessing in disguise. At the office, he was supposed to critically analyse patent applications—to the point of assuming that everything the inventor had mentioned was wrong—and break the theories down to their essence. This seemingly incongruous work for the bent of Einstein's genius actually honed his skills as a theoretical physicist. After all, he wished to come up with a short elegant equation that would unfold the secrets of the universe. He also didn't find the work strenuous, so he could afford to daydream about his different thought experiments. In 1905, along with his doctorate thesis, he published four papers in *Annalen der Physik*. Within a single year, he put forth the quantum theory of light, proved the existence of molecules and atoms, revolutionized the way people understood space and time, devised his famous equation and ultimately became Dr Einstein. His papers reached the desk of the leading physicist Max Planck, who immediately recognized their worth and lauded Einstein's work. His theories changed the course of modern physics, albeit gradually; he expected some academic recognition, perhaps a position at a university, but he was not an overnight success. He continued publishing papers at an amazing rate while maintaining full-time employment—he wrote six in 1906 and 10 the following year. Over the next few years, experiments were conducted that confirmed his theories. He finally entered the university sphere when he was appointed

Privatdozent at Berne in 1908 and Professor Extraordinary at Zurich in 1909—almost a decade after graduating. Prague, Berlin and Princeton are some other places he taught at. In 1916, he published a paper explaining the general theory of relativity, which he is best known for. He divorced Marić, whom he had two sons with, and married his second wife Elsa Einstein in 1919. Einstein had become a German citizen again in 1914 but renounced it once more in 1933 due to the rise of the Nazi Party. In 1940, he took up the citizenship of the United States, where he lived out the remainder of his life. He died at the age of 76 on 18 April 1955.

LASTING LESSON

Life comprises infinite variables. Every day we make thousands of minute decisions that affect our future. Why then do we constantly compare ourselves with others? Or compare our children with their friends, in the hope that our kids will pick on something positive? In fact, it creates friction among them. The struggles that Einstein faced had the potential to completely derail his self-confidence. He was discriminated against, and the schooling system and authority figures he encountered told him he wasn't good enough. He realized that intelligence sprouts in different shades and at different times. Just because he found himself stifled by the formal education system, it didn't mean he wasn't naturally smart or didn't have the ability to learn.

There's a difference between comparison and *inspiration*. We can learn from personalities we look up to and be inspired to work harder and smarter. But comparison only ever leaves us with the negative feelings of envy or discouragement. We may not comply with the standards that we, as a society, have set—and that's alright. Everybody has different innate talents and passions as well as different skillsets to offer. These should be recognized and appreciated in their own right, not through standardized testing or one set meter. As is clear, Einstein himself sometimes didn't do well in academics because he didn't like rote learning. How our lives will unveil cannot be predicted, especially because no two lives are exactly the same—they're like our fingerprints or a zebra's stripes. Everyone has a different kind of intelligence, which may not always be obvious in the current restrictive ways of testing them. So, why not celebrate others' successes rather than try to match up to them? That way, we can focus on our own unique strengths and be positively encouraged to improve upon them as we:

CHOOSE INSPIRATION OVER COMPARISON.

Einstein's Elan

The rising Nazism in Germany found a target in Einstein as he grew successful. They organized book burnings mentioning his work and called his theory of relativity 'Jewish physics'. In 1929, *A Hundred Authors Against Einstein* was published. In response to his theory being denounced in an anti-Semitic attitude, Einstein coolly stated that collecting a hundred scientists was a bit of an overkill because if he were wrong, only one scientist's logic would have been enough to prove it.

REMAIN FLEXIBLE FOR REINVENTION

Vera Wang (b. 1949)

Fashion designer

Reinvention is crucial to survival today and relevant now more than ever. Reinvention, however, requires immense flexibility, an open mind and a creative spirit.

Vera Wang

What do Michelle Obama, Victoria Beckham, Keira Knightley and Charlize Theron have in common? Besides being powerful women in their own right, they have all worn a Vera Wang dress, whether at high-profile events or their weddings. An Asian-American fashion designer known primarily for bridal gowns, Wang owns flagship stores in major cities in the United States, including New York City and Beverly Hills, and also across the world in locations such as Osaka, Beijing, Istanbul, Athens and Sydney. As the go-to designer for all things luxury weddings—especially since she started her lines of engagement rings, invitations and gifting—her net worth is unsurprisingly $460 million. She has been awarded the Council of Fashion Designers of America's 2005 Womenswear Designer of the Year and Geoffrey Beene Lifetime Achievement awards, along with the André Leon

Talley Lifetime Achievement Award from the Savannah College of Art and Design. Epitomizing the celebrity fashion designer, she has appeared in several films and TV shows as herself and written a book on weddings too.

But it was not fashion that originally drove the young Vera Wang; her heart lay in figure skating. Growing up, she dreamt of competing at the Olympics, and it was that aim she devoted all her efforts to. What she learnt along the way ensured that she did not remain hopeless or static when things didn't unfurl according to her expectations. Instead, she switched gears and used it as an opportunity to discover another side to herself.

THE WOMAN BEFORE THE LABEL

Born on 27 June 1949 in New York City, US, Vera Wang has called the city home her entire life. Her parents were born in China and emigrated to the US in the 1940s, where they had Wang and her younger brother. Her father C.C. Wang, an MIT graduate and the son of a Chinese war minister, founded his own company with few friends from university. Wang's mother Florence Wu worked for the United Nations as a translator. In her daughter's eyes, Florence Wu was the foremost style icon since she married the influences of her past in China with the new fashions she discovered in the US. Shopping for the Wangs was a family event, an outing they took together. It didn't matter what they were looking at—clothes, food or cars—they made a day out of evaluating, critiquing and comparing them. Wang's father even followed high fashion and sent his family to Paris to shop the latest trends.

While Wang grew up in a privileged household and

studied at the elite Chapin School, her Chinese roots shaped her work ethic. Her father introduced six-year-old Wang to ice skating when he took her to a frozen lake in Central Park, New York, and strapped her in skates. She fell in love with the activity and began figure skating at the age of eight. Two years later, she was competing at various East Coast championships. For over a decade, she dedicated her life to this dream and lived the existence of an overscheduled child though loving every minute of it. Through it, she learnt more about herself as an individual and perceived metaphors that she related to life. No matter how many times she fell, she had to get up and try again, and she did it because of her love for the sport. It engendered in her an admiration for beauty, clean lines, storytelling and reaching out to people emotionally. It was her escape, but it was also how she expressed herself artistically.

Elegant in its deception of being effortless, figure skating demands mental and physical discipline along with a commitment of time and energy that not everyone can cope with, especially a teenager. Wang found herself on ice for an average of eight hours a day as she was determined on becoming a world-renowned competitor at the Olympics. The rigorous training routine forced her to quit Chapin in her senior year. She eventually found a perfect fit at the Professional Children's School that made special allowances for young athletes like her. She then joined Sarah Lawrence College to gain a liberal arts education while simultaneously pursuing her Olympic dream.

Despite Wang's best efforts, she couldn't juggle academics along with the sport. After all her training and sacrifice, the 17-year-old failed to qualify for the US figure-skating team appearing at the 1968 Olympics. She lost out by a fair margin, and she could see that clearly. She refused to delude herself by living in a fantasy world in which she could qualify next time around, that is, after *four years*. This realization was underscored by her friend Peggy Fleming's performance. To Wang, Fleming was the gifted athlete who came around once in a while, and it dawned on Wang that no matter how hard she tried, she could never ape Fleming's figure-skating skill. The final blow to Wang's house of cards came when Sarah Lawrence College asked her to take an indefinite leave of absence or, in other words, expelled her, because she failed to keep up with her studies. Her circumstances suddenly took a 180-degree turn—whereas once she'd had a shot at her sporting dream and studied at a prestigious institution, now her hope of becoming an Olympic star was shattered and she was kicked to the kerb by her beloved college. She thus went from gliding in the sky to being muddied in deep desolation and was confronted by a crossroads:

Path 1

After having dedicated herself to the sport her entire life, Wang had been forced to accept the bitter truth that she would never achieve her ambition. All those days of working herself bone-tired and sacrificing a regular childhood had resulted in *nothing*. And she was nothing—neither was she an Olympian nor a college student. She had tried her best, and she had failed. More than any teacher or family member, she had disappointed herself. At least she had her family's wealth to fall back on. She didn't *have* to work for her livelihood; she could spend a comfortable life without a career. Why fight fate?

Path 2

Except, the adults Wang had grown up with—her parents—had set an example. They belonged to affluent families, but that didn't stop them from working. There must be a reason to pursue a career other than earning money. And it all clicked in her mind—of course, *passion*. The passion she felt for figure skating was what propelled her. It was clear to her now that the sport was out of the picture, but that didn't mean she had to remain rigid and sink without trying to grasp at another life raft. She didn't need to have everything figured out immediately either; she could take the time to explore other interests and revaluate her options.

Wang found solace in France and immersed herself in Parisian culture—its rich art history, gorgeous architecture, tantalizing food, but most significantly, illustrious fashion famed for its construction and craftsmanship. Paris is where she fell in love with fashion and felt a familiar fire reignite, the kind she had held for skating. Her time in the city reaffirmed her inclination to return to school. At the age of 20, she began her journey anew in an unfamiliar territory. Her second attempt at Sarah Lawrence College was different—she fully committed herself to studies while learning the significance of timing, priorities and reinvention. She attributes the college with providing her a haven by giving her the freedom and flexibility to discover herself. In her junior year, she returned to Paris by enrolling in the college's international programme, and a life in the fashion industry captured her imagination like skating once had. She wished to study fashion design after Sarah Lawrence, but her father told her that he wouldn't pay for any further expensive education and that she should find a job. Upon graduation, she joined *Vogue* to learn more about the industry and became one of the youngest fashion editors to ever work there. She spent over 15 years at the organization and believes that learning on the job gave her the best education about the industry she could have received. But she yearned to create her own products, so she joined Ralph Lauren as a design director in 1987.

Two years into the company and nearing 40, Wang was planning her wedding to Arthur Becker and couldn't find a gown that she thought was appropriate for her age and design aesthetic. Ultimately, she sketched it herself and got it made by someone, and her father realized that there was a gap in the market. Weddings then weren't newsworthy events, and there wasn't much variety in the style of dresses. What Wang had felt must be shared by other brides—the desire to don a dress that suited their individual personalities. Wang's father told her that he would support her business venture if she focused on bridal wear, and she opened her first boutique on Madison Avenue in New York City. Initially, the Vera Wang Bridal House displayed a selection of couture gowns from famous labels, but she honed her design skills and introduced her own collection soon enough. Apart from becoming a dominating presence in the wedding market, she has launched a more affordable ready-to-wear line, Simply Vera, in conjunction with US department store Kohl's. Wang has since then expanded into menswear, fragrances, fashion jewellery, footwear and cosmetics, and she is still going strong at the age of 71. Her now ex-husband and she have two daughters, whom she passed down her love of figure skating to.

LASTING LESSON

Persistence is an aspirational attribute, but in its extreme form, *dogged* persistence can lead to self-delusion, exasperation and dejection. We should of course try our hardest to achieve our aim, though we should remain self-aware enough to know when we have reached our limits because we all have them. It is wonderful when our passion coincides with our career, but we are capable of being passionate about more than one thing. We need to allow ourselves the time, freedom, open-mindedness and, most importantly, *flexibility* to discover different sides of our personality so that we can reinvent ourselves when the situation demands it. We may be fascinated by a certain career choice by the way it looks to us from the outside, but sometimes the realities of those jobs do not rise to our expectations. Even if we find our way into a career that we love, we all go through various transitions— of organizations and industries as well as in our personal and familial lives. Such shifts require us to be flexible as we constantly change due to external circumstances along with inner growth, and we may find ourselves to be completely different people from who we were a decade ago. It is at these points that the power of reinvention comes into play and helps us adapt to dynamic roles. This is not to say that one has to always start afresh and carry none of the learning from previous forms. All of the lessons Vera Wang had learnt as a figure skater came in handy as a fashion designer. Figure skating taught Wang to dust herself off and try again each time she took a fall. But it didn't necessarily mean repeating the same task over and over again, especially when she realized that she had reached the pinnacle of her skating skills. However, she could use the life skills that she had learnt and apply them elsewhere, which is exactly what she did. She also believes the two careers are directly linked in their appreciation of beauty, lines and artistic expression. And just like a figure-skating costume must be attractive as a whole as it is seen from all angles during a performance, she created wedding gowns that were gorgeous on all sides, especially since they're mostly seen from the back during the ceremony. Of course, the discipline she built as an athlete proves useful to her today too when she has to design multiple collections every year, each with its own unique inspiration and theme. Like Wang, we can excel at changing according to ups and downs and explore trails that offshoot from main roads if we:

REMAIN FLEXIBLE FOR REINVENTION.

Wang's Wondrous Wins

Even without figure skating at the Olympics, Vera Wang has managed to be associated with it and the Olympic medals. She designed the costumes of numerous award-winning figure skaters, including Nancy Kerrigan in 1992 and 1994, Michelle Kwan in 1998 and 2002, Evan Lysacek in 2010 and Nathan Chen in 2018. They all won medals wearing Wang's designs. In 2009, she was inducted by her country into the US Figure Skating Hall of Fame for her contribution to the sport as a costume designer.

CRITICS AREN'T ALWAYS RIGHT

The Beatles (circa 1957–1970)

Band

You don't need anybody to tell you who you are or what you are.

John Lennon

Fifty years after their last performance, The Beatles continue to be adored the world over and we are yet to see a cultural phenomenon like them again. Also known as the Fab Four, the band achieved commercial success with members John Lennon (9 October 1940-8 December 1980), Paul McCartney (b. 18 June 1942), George Harrison (25 February 1943-29 November 2001) and Ringo Starr (b. 7 July 1940). Their appeal has never been restricted to an age group, so those who witnessed The Beatles in action and the ones born long after the band was dissolved can be seen sporting Beatles T-shirts and quoting lyrics from songs such as 'Yesterday', 'Let It Be', 'Hey Jude' and 'I Want to Hold Your Hand'. Funnily, the bestselling music act of all time in the United States happens to be this British band, topping even the likes of Michael Jackson and Elvis Presley with a certified 183 million album sales. Besides seven Grammy wins and an Oscar for Best Original Song, all four members of the band received Member of the Most Excellent Order of the British Empire (MBE) medals in 1965, and Paul McCartney and Ringo Starr were knighted in 1997 and 2018, respectively. They also starred in a few films and, in 1968, launched their own multimedia company, Apple Corps (pronounced as 'apple core'—a pun on the fruit and not to be mistaken with the electronics company).

The sheer number of documentaries and biographies encapsulating their careers and lives is astonishing considering The Beatles were active with a record deal for just eight years. The band's short lifespan has not dimmed the adulation of its dedicated and ever-growing fan base, although critics initially labelled their music 'rubbish.'

THE BOYS BEFORE BEATLEMANIA

Born within a few years of each other in Liverpool, United Kingdom, the Fab Four didn't grow up in the most affluent of backgrounds. As a major port, Liverpool was a target for air raids in World War II. Due to the war and its after-effects, people endured hard times with food rationing.

James Paul McCartney and George Harrison resided close by, knew each other from a young age and came from similar working-class roots. McCartney's mother was a midwife and his father worked in the cotton trade and played a few instruments himself. He bought his son a trumpet that McCartney later traded for a guitar since he couldn't sing while playing the brass instrument. Harrison's father was a bus conductor and his mother a shop assistant who adored music as well. They stayed in a house with no electricity; the lone source of heat was coal fire, and the toilet was in the backyard. Harrison bought his first guitar when he was about 13.

The father of Ringo Starr—or Richard Starkey—baked cakes, so his family always had sugar during the war, which was a great luxury at the time. His father left when Starr was three, so his mother had to take up several jobs to support the family. He was a sickly kid and spent a chunk of his childhood in the hospital. The doctors in fact said he wouldn't live long.

John Winston Lennon grew up in slightly better conditions, but as a result of his parents' separation, he was sent to live with his aunt at age five. He had great love for his mother, who taught Lennon the banjo from which he progressed to the guitar.

Most of The Beatles came from broken homes or mourned the deaths of loved ones. One of the things that initially bonded McCartney and Lennon was the loss of their mothers in their teen years due to complications with cancer and a road accident, respectively. The other thing that flared their kinship was songwriting; in those days, it was rare for groups to write and compose their music or play their own instruments. Most acts that erupted in the UK were diluted copies of American icons like Elvis and Frank Sinatra. The famous writing partnership began due to a chance meeting at a fete in 1957 where Lennon was performing with his group, The Quarry Men. McCartney picked up Lennon's guitar backstage and played a song. He knew all the lyrics, which impressed Lennon terribly. McCartney joined the band soon after that. Records, song lyrics, information about music theory—all that is easily available today was scarce in 1950s England. While performing covers of famous artists, young Lennon sometimes sang lyrics of other songs since he didn't know the original words, and in order to learn a guitar chord, the boys travelled to the other end of the city in search of someone who did! They both played the guitar but weren't confident enough to do solos, so to fill the role of lead guitarist, McCartney suggested Harrison. He was a bit younger than the others and looked even more so. But he wowed the older kids with his guitar skills in an audition that took place on the top tier of a double-decker bus late one night. Originally, Stuart Sutcliffe—a friend of Lennon from the Liverpool College of Art, which he attended—joined the band as its bassist. They booked performances in Hamburg, Germany, in 1960 and took on Pete Best as their drummer.

The band went through a few name changes (including 'The Silver Beetles'), but around this time landed upon the one we remember them by. In Hamburg, they improved upon their stage presence as they played in clubs and bars while earning just enough to feed themselves and living in a closet-sized room. Meanwhile, Ringo Starr played drums for another Liverpudlian band called Rory Storm and the Hurricanes, which also went to Hamburg and was one of the first rock 'n' roll bands to emerge from the city. It was discovered in November 1960 that, at 17, Harrison was underage to play at nightclubs, and their contract was terminated. The authorities deported him. Disheartened Harrison was surprised to find McCartney and Best—who had set fire to an object as a prank and were apprehended—awaiting Harrison in Liverpool. Lennon returned in a few days too, leaving Sutcliffe behind with his new German girlfriend. McCartney eventually shifted to the bass. On another trip to Hamburg in 1961, The Beatles excitedly thought that they had been scouted by a German producer, only to realize that he wanted them to provide backup to Tony Sheridan for the song My Bonnie. As fate would have it, a customer at one of Brian Epstein's family-owned record shops asked for the song, which is how he first heard of The Beatles. He went to watch them perform live in Liverpool and detected a star quality even in their unpolished form. He offered to manage the group and is now often referred to as the 'fifth Beatle'. Quickly scoring them more performances and radio appearances, he also switched their black-leather look to the suits of the early Beatles era.

On New Year's Eve 1961, the band travelled to London to audition for Decca Records on the first day of 1962. Exhausted from the long drive, they still tried to perform their best and recorded 15 songs for the audition. Here's the kicker—The Beatles, yes, *The Beatles*, were passed over for another act that history reveals were no rival to the most influential band on this planet. Except, the boys didn't have the privilege we do of knowing how things turned out eventually and faced a crossroads:

Path 1

This was it. This was the proverbial straw that broke the camel's back. For how long were the four boys going to chase dreams that seemed just that—*dreams*? Especially now when music bigwigs heard what they could do and still didn't think them good enough to invest in? Dick Rowe, a senior employee in the company, supposedly told Epstein that guitar groups were on the way out. If the boys had any sense at all, they would listen to insiders of the industry that they were trying to crack and either change their act completely or stick to what they'd been doing thus far—play local venues in Liverpool. Perhaps Lennon's Aunt Mimi had been right when she reportedly told him that playing guitar was fine but had no potential for generating money.

Path 2

Dick Rowe and the others at Decca Records were nothing but human, and their decision wasn't prophesized by a higher power or etched in stone. Taste is so subjective, especially when it comes to the arts. The Beatles were weird because they *chose* to do something different, something new. And not everybody had to love it or even understand it. There must have been a reason Epstein picked them and people in Liverpool as well as Germany enjoyed their music. The band had to have faith in their own vision and accept that if they were attempting to do something out of the ordinary, they were going to come across naysayers.

Decca Records may have rejected The Beatles, but Epstein shopped the recorded songs around. Frustrated, he turned to what he might have perceived as his worst option—a comedy label, Parlophone Records, a subsidiary of EMI. Its Artists and Repertoire head, George Martin, took the band on but had a stipulation regarding changing the drummer, and that's how Ringo Starr came on board and completed the family. Martin wasn't entirely impressed with the band at first as their sound was so new and unexpected. The concept of the band baffled him, and he tried figuring out who the lead singer would be since all members of the band sang. Gradually, he chose to accept them as what they were—a group—though Lennon and McCartney usually took lead on the vocals and lyric-writing. They released their first record, 'Love Me Do', which became a popular track and forced EMI to be more open to the band from there on out. Martin asked them if they had a song that could potentially reach the top spot, and Lennon presented 'Please Please Me', which did reach number one and was the title of their debut album. Their music also climbed the charts in other countries, but in the US in even the mid-1960s, critics called their music awful. There was no denying that they were loved by the fans, especially considering that The Beatles performed for a crowd of over 55,000 in New York City in 1965 and couldn't hear themselves play because the crowd screeched throughout. They were a prolific band since Epstein and Martin had a fixed plan that ensured they released a single every three months and an album every six. Their music developed over the years as they experimented with other genres, styles and influences, and their work was trailblazing and trendsetting—they even brought the sitar into mainstream pop and were among the first to delve into psychedelic music.

Epstein passed away unexpectedly at age 32 in 1967 and the band broke up in 1970. All four of them were successful as individual artists post the band as well. Lennon was sadly shot and killed in 1980 by a disturbed fan. Harrison was likewise attacked and stabbed by a fan who broke into his house in 1999. He survived the assault but passed away after a long battle with cancer in 2001. McCartney and Starr perform and release music even today.

LASTING LESSON

Being critiqued is a tricky spot to be in. We all want to showcase our work or our abilities and receive feedback from people whose opinions we can trust—whether they are our well-wishers or they're knowledgeable about the relevant field. That is a great way to improve our skills, especially if the project we're working on is meant to be appreciated by the masses and isn't for our personal enjoyment. Yet there's something to be said of individual tastes and the expectations people have. Our preferences and the parameters in which we understand and appreciate things are, to a large extent, set by observing what is already out there. But how would this come into play if the project lay outside familiar settings? Take, for example, the case of Alexander Graham Bell's invention, the telephone. Western Union considered it merely a toy and refused to purchase its patent for $100,000. They soon realized their mistake, of course.

While attempting something new, we always run the risk of alienating and discomforting some people, but that just means they're not the target audience or they haven't become so *yet*. Whether we're trying to introduce new processes at work that we believe could improve the functioning of the organization or experimenting with a new technique of applying paint to a canvas, we're probably going to run into roadblocks in the form of those who are set in their ways. Though if no one takes risks, how would we as a society ever evolve? And it is obvious that among us exist those outliers and dreamers, since we continue to see developments in art, culture, science and philosophy. Yes, there is a fine line between carefully analysing our critics' feedback and self-delusion or bullheadedness, but the way to ensure that we experiment and advance is by believing that:

CRITICS AREN'T ALWAYS RIGHT.

The Beatles and Bharat

In 1967, The Beatles attended a retreat on Transcendental Meditation headed by Maharishi Mahesh Yogi in Wales, UK. However, their time there was cut short due to the news of Epstein's death. They, along with their respective wives or girlfriends, later travelled to Rishikesh to Maharishi's ashram for a meditation course. The enormous press related to this event exposed the West to concepts in Indian spirituality. This was also one of the band's most inspired periods as they reportedly wrote close to 50 songs. The band left with different attitudes, especially because of the allegations against Maharishi for displaying inappropriate behaviour towards the women. This did not allay George Harrison's interest in Indian spirituality and music though. He had come across the sitar in the band's 1965 film, *Help!*, and was intrigued by Indian classical music. He'd picked up the instrument, which features in some of their songs, and had met Pandit Ravi Shankar in 1966. The late sitar maestro taught Harrison, and they collaborated on a few projects, including the 1971 Concert for Bangladesh and the four-disc *Collaborations* compilation.

MASTER TRADES RELEVANT TO THE JOB

Michael Jordan (b. 1963)

Basketball player

Even though I knew how hard I worked on defence, all anyone noticed was the way I scored. So, that made me work even harder to get that recognition as a complete player.

Michael Jordan

One doesn't have to be a fan of basketball to know who Michael Jordan is. Considered one of the greatest athletes to have ever lived, Jordan played a huge role in popularizing the sport and the National Basketball Association (NBA) in the 1980s and 1990s. Under his leadership, the Chicago Bulls won six NBA championships in 1991–1993 and 1996–1998, and he won several accolades in the process, including Rookie of the Year, Most Valuable Player (MVP), Defensive Player of the Year and All-Star MVP awards. He's also had a successful stint in endorsing products, most popularly Nike's Air Jordan shoes. At the height of his career, his fame was akin to a rock star's—crowds waited for hours to catch a glimpse of him on his travels and enough news crews surrounded his house to give the impression that it was a film set. There are numerous documentaries about him, and he has forayed into Hollywood as well. Not just *anybody* can star in a movie alongside iconic Looney Tunes characters Bugs Bunny and Daffy Duck, but Jordan accomplished that in the much-loved *Space Jam*. It mustn't come as a revelation then that he was the first NBA player to join the ranks of billionaires and continues to be counted among the top 10 Black billionaires of the world.

Anyone watching Michael Jordan's graceful movements and almost-flights on the court would believe he was born to play the sport, but even he was cut from his high school basketball team. The choice he made then and later in his career pushed him to superstardom and earned him the label of basketball's Greatest of All Time, or G.O.A.T.

THE MAN WHO WOULD BE THE G.O.A.T.

Born in Brooklyn, New York, in the United States on 17 February 1963, Michael Jordan is the fourth-born in a family of five children. His mother Deloris worked as a bank teller and his father James was an equipment supervisor. When Jordan was a toddler, the family moved to Wilmington, North Carolina, and resided there throughout his childhood. Father and son bonded over their shared love of baseball, but it was his older brother Larry whom young Jordan idolized. He wanted to be just like his brother, and Larry loved playing basketball. Jordan's own passion for it was ignited through pick-up games with Larry, and the pair were often found on the court their father had built in the backyard. Larry usually beat his brother, which made Jordan that much more eager to improve in the hope of one day toppling his idol. Jordan believed that if he could defeat his brother, he could defeat anyone. As his skills grew over the years, so did his height, until he towered over Larry and finally bested him one day.

While Jordan dabbled in different sports at high school, basketball was his true love. In the tenth grade, he tried out for the varsity (equivalent to the school team in India) basketball team but wasn't selected by the coach. At 5'11", Jordan was reportedly too short for the team and his skills weren't polished enough, even though he showed promise. He was disappointed but determined as ever. Over the course of the year, Jordan worked out, enhanced his game and shone in the junior varsity team. Whenever the going got tough, he closed his eyes and visualized the varsity team list without his name on it and strove harder. Fortunately, he also shot up by four inches. He was finally chosen for varsity and instantly became the school's top player. He'd come a long way from the rejection and was now the favourite for recruiters of several college basketball programmes. Jordan chose the scholarship offered by the University of South Carolina as it had a rich basketball tradition. Some scepticism regarding his abilities was still rife though. The people in his school thought he'd sit on the bench for four years and return to work in the town. He shattered their assumptions when the legendary Coach Dean Smith chose Jordan to play on the team in his first year. At the 1982 national championship game against the Georgetown team led by his future rival Patrick Ewing, Jordan grabbed eyeballs by making the winning jump-shot— the biggest in the history of the National Collegiate Athletic Association (NCAA). This shot won Smith his first NCAA victory and was a turning point in Jordan's career. In his second year, *The Sporting News* named him College Player of the Year. He received the same title the following season along with the Naismith College Player of the Year and John R. Wooden awards. A year before completing his Bachelor's degree in geography, he left to play pro basketball. But he first made his global debut at the 1984 Olympics as a part of the US team and took the gold medal. He was drafted by the Chicago Bulls, and thus began his illustrious career at the NBA.

Named Rookie of the Year in his first NBA season, Jordan quickly became a fan-favourite. He seemed to have been born for not only the game but the life of an NBA player and the fame that accompanied it—he came across as open and outgoing, and he especially liked interacting with his younger fans. As a cultural icon, everything he did set a new trend. He was among the first athletes to shave his head, which is now a common sight in basketball. Before him, players wore tight-fitting mid-thigh shorts, but he preferred longer, looser ones because, as legend has it, he liked wearing his college basketball shorts underneath. Now when someone mentions 'basketball shorts', the baggier one is precisely what we picture.

Jordan's slam dunk abilities had everyone captivated. He moved so fast that it appeared he was committing a foul by travelling, and his high jumps could almost make a viewer believe Jordan could fly. This gave rise to the nicknames 'Air Jordan' and 'His Airness'. While his stardom as a scorer increased, so did rumours that he was a selfish player, focused on personal high scores and not the team's win. Jordan also wasn't reputed for his defence and passing skills. These talks were substantiated by the fact that though the

Chicago Bulls were faring better since he joined the team, they were still nowhere near achieving the championship. Early on in Jordan's career, people likened him to all-time-greats Larry Bird and Earvin 'Magic' Johnson. However, it wasn't a true comparison—unlike them, he hadn't led his team to any championship wins. This is how Jordan sprang upon a crossroads that would shape his skills as a player and impact his team's fate:

Path 1

Michael Jordan knew how to slam dunk—no one could deny that. He had won so many solo awards for his performances and enough glory to single him out in the media and among basketball fans everywhere. He was a force of nature near the basket, and he tried his best to score as many points as he could *for his team* so that they would win games. After all, he was supposed to be the scorer and not only did he do his job, he excelled at it. What else could anyone ask for?

Path 2

Usually, Jordan played as a shooting guard, who must also have good defensive skills. And basketball was a *team* sport—he had to pass the ball and be able to rely on his teammates to score as well. Why not improve those skills to become an all-rounder? Then he could support his team wherever they needed him, even if it was with the two skills that didn't come naturally to him. Sure, individual awards existed, but none held the weight of the championship and he alone couldn't win it. He had to claim it so that he could be worthy of being counted among the all-time greats.

A fire rose in Jordan to disprove all those who had ever said he was a one-trick pony. They wanted to see better defence and passing? Jordan would work day and night on those aspects so that he would no longer lag behind the others. In fact, he used his leaping ability—the one that helped with those magnificent slam dunks—to block shots from the opposing team and his quick reflexes to steal the ball from them. His smart plays and hard work bore him results, and he won the Defensive Player of the Year title in 1988 along with that of the MVP, becoming the first player to nab both titles in the same season. The next year, he married Juanita Vanoy, whom he would have three children with.

In the 1986–1987 off season, Chicago Bulls had begun forming a high-calibre team by enlisting other talented players. Three years later, the Bulls brought in a new coach who instituted a different play that gave all five members of the team equal opportunity to score while still providing Jordan the space to improvise his own shot. Each year the Bulls faced obstacles in their path to the championship— obstacles they learnt from to improve their game. Gradually, they inched in closer and closer to the title until 1991 when they finally won their first championship.

The Chicago Bulls successfully defended their position over the next two years. Jordan was a key figure in what came to be known as the 'Dream Team' that participated in the 1992 Olympics and claimed the gold. The following year, Jordan announced what would be his first retirement from basketball. He left the game to try his hand at baseball, where he was an adequate if not spectacular performer. In 1995, he revealed that he was returning to basketball with the short press release that said it all: 'I'm back.' He led the Bulls to three more championships and retired from basketball again in 1999. From 2001 to 2003, he briefly returned to the game by playing for the Washington Wizards. He kept his relationship with the NBA alive by buying a controlling interest in the Charlotte Bobcats (now the Charlotte Hornets) in 2010, thus becoming the first former player to become a majority owner in the NBA. After separating from Vanoy in 2006, he married Yvette Prieto in 2014 and has a set of twins with her.

LASTING LESSON

We are all born with some innate talent or inclination. Since we usually enjoy doing things that we're good at, they become our focus. Why shouldn't they, especially because they come easier to us? It just makes sense to base our work around our interests, which is why so many take aptitude tests to gauge what career paths would best suit their skillsets and personalities. Practically, however, every project requires a combination of skills. Although some of them may be foreign to us, they are significant in getting the end result we want. For example, one's talents may lie in a creative field like painting, so they choose to make a career out of it. To do so, they also have to excel at organizing tasks, time management to meet deadlines and even networking to make the required contacts to receive commissions, have their artwork showcased in galleries and sell their work. These traits may not come naturally to the painter, but without them, the artist would have a hard time converting their innate talent into their career. This becomes especially important when we're leading a team. The manager's job isn't to bark orders but to direct their team's efforts towards a goal. For this, the leader would have to be knowledgeable of every aspect of the work involved, perhaps not to the extent to which the team members would be specialists of their fields, but enough to delegate and look out for errors. Jordan was the captain of his team and he excelled at one skill, scoring, but that wasn't enough. We've heard the old adage, 'Jack of all trades, master of none.' Jordan's lasting lesson doesn't tell us to become a *jack* of *all* trades. He had to master the few skills required to be a well-rounded player and thus galvanize his team to win championships. And we can become all-rounders of our fields as well if we:

MASTER TRADES RELEVANT TO THE JOB.

Michael's Moving Moment

One of the reasons that Jordan first retired from basketball and pursued baseball was to honour his late father's memory and fulfil his wish. His father was unfortunately killed in an armed robbery in 1993. He thought Jordan could excel at two sports—basketball and baseball. However, this was not to be, and Jordan wouldn't stand out as a baseball player. He returned to basketball to once again play for the Chicago Bulls, and the day he recaptured the championship for his team in 1996 happened to be Father's Day. His triumph was clear in the moment when he lay on the court, cradling the ball and crying.

MORE THAN ONE ROUTE LEADS TO TRIUMPH

Steven Spielberg (b. 1946)

Hollywood director and producer

I think rules tend to stagger and topple people who really dream.

Steven Spielberg

The world received some of the most iconic Hollywood movies of the past 50 years—*Jaws, E.T. the Extra-Terrestrial, Jurassic Park,* the *Indiana Jones* series, the *Back to the Future* trilogy, *Schindler's List* and *Lincoln*—all because a 12-year-old Steven Spielberg loved making home movies. A member of the 'Movie Brats' collective that included other film geniuses such as George Lucas, Martin Scorsese and Francis Ford Coppola, Spielberg was adamant on injecting his own aesthetic into Hollywood. Whether he was dealing with robotic sharks, CGI dinosaurs, science-fiction worlds, historical dramas or animated features, Spielberg brought a sense of childlike wonder and authentic emotion to his varied subjects. Best known as a director, he has also written for screen, produced movies and co-founded two production companies, Amblin Entertainment and DreamWorks. His work has been recognized with numerous accolades such as the Oscar, Golden Globe, Emmy, BAFTA, the Presidential Medal of Freedom and a few honorary doctorates from the likes of Harvard and Yale. Considered the most commercially successful director on earth, Spielberg was unsurprisingly the first to hit the $10 billion mark at the global box office.

Spielberg dreamt of creating huge hits from a young age. In order to achieve this, he set out with a vision to make a thrilling monster flick, but it didn't pan out as planned. The smart intuitive choice he made in the face of that shock is the reason he has become one of the most recognizable moviemakers today.

THE MAN IN THE DIRECTOR'S SEAT

Though Steven Allan Spielberg was born in Ohio in the United States on 18 December 1946, he spent most of his formative years in the suburbs of Phoenix, Arizona. His mother Leah was a concert pianist and restauranteur and his father Arnold an electrical engineer who worked in computing. They had three other children, all girls.

At school, Spielberg was picked on for his Jewish faith. Never the sports buff or class topper, he found an escape in films. Around the age of five, he went to the cinema for the first time and watched a train-crash sequence that left a lasting impression on him. He asked his father for an electric train set and continued collecting them over the next few years. When he was 12, he recalled the movie and began colliding two of the trains in order to recreate the crash scene, but the trains kept breaking. His father eventually warned Spielberg that if he broke them again, his entire set would be confiscated. Backed into a corner, he was forced to think on his feet. He fetched his father's 8 mm Kodak movie camera and recorded the two trains approaching each other, thus capturing their moment of impact, so he could watch it to his heart's content. Fortunately, the toy trains weren't damaged, and he ended up with his first movie. He wondered what else he could do with the camera. To earn the photography merit badge as a Boy Scout, he made a short Western film, enlisting his sisters and friends as actors. Their laughter and positive response to the viewing thrilled him, and he decided then and there to pursue filmmaking so he could continue receiving feedback and affirmation for his work. He made other short films, including a war movie for which he snuck into a nearby airport and shot old aircrafts. At age 17, he made his first feature-length movie *Firelight* on a budget of $400. It was shown at a local theatre, and enough people showed up for Spielberg to make a profit of $100.

Spielberg not only experimented and learnt with his own devices, he also observed others at work. During a summer vacation, Spielberg took an official tour of Universal Studios in Hollywood. During a toilet break that the visitors received, he hid in a bathroom until everyone else cleared out. Then he proceeded to roam around, watching various TV and movie shootings. He managed to enter the studios for three months, wearing a coat and tie and carrying a briefcase in an attempt to look like one of the employees. He once snuck into Alfred Hitchcock's set but was caught and asked to leave. Legend has it that Spielberg even occupied an empty office and got his own telephone line.

Longing to formally study the craft, Spielberg applied to the film school at the University of Southern California (USC). Due to his low academic scores, he was denied admission.

He finally joined California State University, Long Beach, but considers the time he spent at Universal Studios his real education. He made a short film, *Amblin'*, which found its way to the desk of a Universal executive who was so impressed by it that he offered Spielberg a seven-year directing contract. It was unheard of at the time for a young newcomer to be offered such a long-term deal, so of course Spielberg jumped at the chance and left his college education midway. One of his first jobs was to direct the acclaimed Joan Crawford for a TV episode, who was originally put off by a fresh face in his early twenties trying to tell her what to do on set but quickly recognized his talent. He directed a few more episodes until he heard that *Duel*—a TV movie based on a short story that he liked—was to be made soon, and he threw his hat in the ring for the director's seat. *Duel* was received well, and he went on to direct a few more TV movies. His first feature film was the 1974 *The Sugarland Express*. While it didn't do wonders at the box office, critics responded positively.

The turning point in Spielberg's life came in 1975 when he was chosen to direct *Jaws*, a thriller-horror about an enormous human-eating shark. This could be his big break, and Spielberg wanted to do things differently. Instead of shooting in the tanks at the studios or on lakes, he would do so in the open ocean for the sake of authenticity. He, along with the cast, crew and the animatronic shark, set off to Martha's Vineyard. He actually got three sharks made, at a cost of $150,000 *each*, and they were quite sophisticated for the time. Tourists from all over gathered about, filling 20 boats, waiting with bated breath to watch the shark come shooting headfirst out of the water. When Spielberg and his team pressed the button, it shot out tail-first and left the tourists disappointed and Spielberg nervous. The robot sharks hadn't been tested in ocean water, and the salt affected their mechanism. As if that wasn't bad enough, Spielberg had committed the rookie mistake of not realizing that the wind, water's currents and colour changes of the ocean would impact the shooting. He was going over budget and time, and his main villain wouldn't figuratively come out of its trailer. Stuck in a set where everything seemed to be going wrong, Spielberg found himself at a crossroads:

Path 1

Spielberg had a fixed plan for how the movie would turn out. He'd pictured it all, and his creative vision must be fulfilled. This was going to be the smash hit of the summer and make him a household name. Everything had to be perfect. There was absolutely no question about it; he needed the shark—it was the Godzilla to his monster movie. After all, how could he make a shark movie *without* the shark? And he had paid close to half a million dollars for the robots, so he just needed to wait until they got fixed.

Path 2

He was already running behind schedule and the studio was getting impatient. If he refused to budge from his original vision and wasted any more time or resources, he could be fired. Then this golden opportunity would slip right through his fingers. No, he had to think of another way out. He could shoot the scenes that didn't involve the shark in the meantime and hope the robots would get fixed by the time they were done. If not... well, then he would come up with another plan.

Little did Spielberg know that his decision to make the best of the circumstances would lead him to create a movie that put him on the map and invent an entirely new category—the summer blockbuster. The sharks didn't get fixed throughout the shooting, and Spielberg had to resort to other methods to convey the shark's presence in most of the movie. As a creative problem-solver who realized there were alternate means to approach a difficult situation, he came up with an unexpected idea to tackle this particular issue. He used the natural setting he was in, the one that was making the filming process difficult. He relied on motions of the water to create a sense of disarray, moving objects such as barrels to imply the shark's advances, but most significantly, music. The slow-building menace of the *dun-dun, dun-dun, dun-dun, bom, bom, bom, bom* notes crafted by John Williams signalled the presence and proximity of the shark as well as the rising tension. The overall impact was that of a psychological terror of the unseen. The way Spielberg dealt with suspense in *Jaws* has been likened to Hitchcock's skill in his horror flicks. Spielberg himself stated that if the animatronic sharks hadn't gone awry, *Jaws* would have been an entirely different movie and probably not much of a success. And what a success it was! It broke all box-office records of the time and made Spielberg a millionaire many times over. Although the movie budget was double of what had been slotted and it was shot over almost 160 days as opposed to the scheduled 55, the huge profits it made gave Spielberg the pass to work on any movie he wished for.

In 1985, Spielberg married Amy Irving and had a son with her, but they separated four years later, and he married Kate Capshaw in 1991. The couple shares six children.

Though Spielberg faced a few struggles later on, with flops such as *1941*, overall he's had an immensely successful career and is today worth an estimated $3.7 billion (though some sources say it may be as high as $6.5 billion). He has made a career working on a wide range of genres and subjects and is considered one of the pioneers of the New Hollywood era.

LASTING LESSON

Once we have figured out our goals—whether they are short or long term—the next step is to sketch a path towards achieving them. We do so by thinking of situations playing out in a certain manner, which they don't always do because life is random. There are no rules behind its workings. That may be terrifying to consider, but it's also *liberating*—because it implies there is no one right way to do things. The rules that do exist should be looked upon as guidelines offered by someone who has ventured into the deep unknown and relayed their trajectory for others, much like an explorer. This doesn't necessarily mean no other routes exist. It is great to be inspired by someone. However, before we place them on a pedestal and think that the way they went about achieving success is the *only* way, we need to consider the variables in all our lives. If the billions of people alive can lead billions of different lives, why can't there be billions of different methods to approach things? Some such as Lucas, Coppola and Scorsese meet their professional goals by pursuing the relevant education and working their way up the ladder. Others, like Spielberg, drop out of college and fine-tune their craft on the job. Even our bodies are different and require specific approaches to remain healthy.

For some, weight training might work, while others may need more cardiovascular exercises. The kind of optimal diet that would suit a body varies too. The end goal is the same—to be fit and healthy—but there are so many techniques to reach that state. It doesn't make much sense to standardize particular methods then. A truer picture would be painted by visualizing our journeys and the possible paths we can take as the network of nerves in our bodies. Paths A, B, C—all the way to infinite—can lead us to our aims, though some may take longer or be more strenuous. We can fulfil our goals if we remember to not stay rigid to a single method because:

MORE THAN ONE ROUTE LEADS TO TRIUMPH.

Spielberg and Shoah Survivors

In 1993, while working on *Schindler's List*—the black-and-white movie about Nazi prison camps and how Oskar Schindler managed to save the lives of over a thousand Jews—Spielberg spoke to many survivors of the Holocaust. Wanting to record their testimonies because he felt these stories needed to be told, he founded the USC Shoah Foundation. This vision has expanded over the years to include the histories of survivors of the 1994 Rwandan Tutsi Genocide, the 1937 Nanjing Massacre and the Guatemalan Genocide, among others. The archive now contains over 55,000 video testimonies.

PROSPERITY DOES NOT EQUAL SUCCESS

Ratan Tata (b. 1937)

Chairman of Tata Trusts and
former Chairman of Tata Sons

You shouldn't really consider yourself successful based on the prosperity you gain for yourself. But you should go home at night feeling satisfied if you have made a difference.

Ratan Tata

Beloved by an entire nation, Ratan Tata is one of the most iconic business leaders to have emerged from India. Possessing the rare combination of business acumen and philanthropic interests, he took the rich legacy of the Tatas to newer heights. For 21 years, he served as the chairman of Tata Sons, the principal investment holding company of Tata Group that comprises the likes of Tata Steel, Tata Consultancy Services, Tata Motors and Indian Hotels. Altogether, their revenue adds up to $110 billion and employs 700,000 people in all continents barring Antarctica. Retiring as chairman emeritus, he currently heads Tata Trusts—a philanthropic body dating back to 1892—as its chairman.

Institutions such as the University of Cambridge, Carnegie Mellon University and Indian Institute of Technology have awarded him honorary doctorates, and he has been presented the Padma Bhushan and Padma Vibhushan. His achievements have been recognized by foreign governments too—he was the first Indian since the nation became a republic to receive the Knight Grand Cross of the Order of the British Empire, and the French government conferred on him the title of Commander of the Legion of Honour.

One would assume that being born with the well-known surname, Tata would've glided through life into the chairman's seat. Yet his journey didn't always include fancy cars and fancier designations, and the grace and integrity that he displayed through it all are among his foremost attributes today as well.

BEFORE THE BUSINESS ICON

Ratan Naval Tata was born in Mumbai in the renowned Parsi industrialist family on 28 December 1937. His parents Naval Tata (the adopted son of Sir Ratan Tata) and Soonoo Tata separated in the mid-1940s, and both went on to have second marriages. Tata and his younger brother were brought up by their grandmother, Lady Navajbai, who played an influential role in their formative years. She indulged her grandsons but balanced it with discipline: Tata was pushed towards excellence and learnt the piano and played cricket growing up. She lived by a strict moral code and also ingrained that in the boys.

In Mumbai, Tata split his education between The Campion School and The Cathedral and John Connon School. Though many of his classmates belonged to affluent households, Tata was embarrassed whenever his grandmother's opulent Rolls-Royce picked him up from school, preferring to walk home instead. At age 15, he left for the United States, where he attended prep school before gaining admission to the prestigious Cornell University in New York. Now and again, he ran into the then-chairman of Tata Sons, J.R.D. Tata, but the two shared a formal relationship. They finally bonded over their love of flying, a skill Tata had learnt at a young age in Mumbai. Excitedly awaiting his first solo flight, Tata fulfilled his wish the day he reached the legal age, his seventeenth birthday. Another love fostered in his college days was the one for cars: Mercedes-Benz had a joint venture with Telco (now Tata Motors) in India to manufacture trucks, and Tata's family sent him a sleek black Mercedes car, which he looked after so well that it remained spotless.

It wasn't all fun and games though. Foreign currency was hard to come by due to some RBI restrictions, so Tata washed planes at the airport to meet his living expenses or gain access to more flying time. His father wished for him to become a mechanical engineer, which is why Tata pursued the course although he didn't enjoy it. His interest was piqued by architecture, which taught him how to approach problems creatively. To his father's displeasure, he switched streams at the end of his second year. The change clearly suited him as he was placed among the top students in class. In 1962, he bid farewell to Cornell after completing a five-year architecture degree and a two-year structural engineering programme. Having every intention to settle in the US, he moved to Los Angeles to join an architecture firm. Then he received word that his grandmother's health was on the decline. For the love he bore the matriarch who raised him, he uprooted himself from the country he had spent a decade in and returned to India.

Tata reached India with an appointment letter in hand from IBM but was told by J.R.D. that if he was going to be in the country, he should work at Tata Sons. Consequently, Tata was shipped off to Jamshedpur with no clue of what he was getting into, only to find out that he had been designated to the shop floor of Telco. Now the tides had turned: instead of being chauffeured in a luxurious Rolls-Royce or driving one of his beloved cars, the automobile aficionado was informed he should use a bicycle for transportation. In a rebellion mirroring the one from his childhood, he walked to work every day. Part of his six-month apprenticeship involved shovelling limestone and working blast furnaces, and often he was left to his own devices without any definite directions. He felt at a loss, but in retrospect it seemed to provide him a tremendous learning experience as he formed a wide knowledge base. Next, he was placed in an automotive plant for trucks and later at Tisco (now Tata Steel). He moved through various assignments until he finally worked his way up to the post of technical assistant to the managing director. Afterwards, he was sent to Australia to handle a joint venture for the company, for which he spent six months in Sydney. When he returned, he refused to head back to Jamshedpur. But his journey wasn't about to get any easier.

In an effort to explore other fields, Tata joined Tata Consultancy Services. At the time, it focused on converting paper documents to processable punch cards. He heard talk that the company would be venturing into the manufacture of coloured television sets, and as an avid fan of new technology, he was excited at the prospect. However, nothing became of this. In 1971, he moved to one of the toughest projects he has worked upon, one that everyone stayed away from: The National Radio and Electronics Company (Nelco). As director-in-charge of Nelco, he was entrusted with the task of saving it from financial doom since its losses equalled its capital. Things were beginning to turn around, but then labour troubles began and the Emergency struck. The company ultimately shut down its production of consumer electronics, thus marking a 'failure' in Tata's file and forcing him at a crossroads:

Path 1

Tata had been moving from one location to another, one job to the next with less-than-optimum results. Either he wasn't taken seriously and left to fend for himself or given impossible tasks. In a uniquely paradoxical situation, he was forced to constantly prove himself worthy of his name, yet none expected him to be J.R.D.'s successor since he didn't have any major successes to boast of. What was he doing back in India anyway? He had been happy in the US, with friends and a stable profession. The person he had returned for, his grandmother, had passed away in 1965, so there was nothing holding him back—he could go back to the US.

Path 2

It's true that Tata had returned for his grandmother's sake and contemplated heading back to the US a few times, but obviously something else was keeping him in India—perhaps, the challenges? Although his hard work didn't look like obvious great successes as Nelco was far from being a shining star among the Tata companies, he had rescued it from drowning under the burden of heavy losses. To the outsider it may not seem like a remarkable feat, but Tata knew the huge difference that lay between not knowing whether they could make the payroll next month and becoming a healthy organization that paid dividends. The aims with which he conducted his business and himself mattered to him, even if they didn't translate to paper.

Upon first reaching Nelco, Tata saw a brighter future for the company and wanted to change its direction so that it aligned with where the times were headed. He faced resistance from the management and couldn't get the capital he needed to achieve those aims. He worked within the available means and managed to convert Nelco's two per cent market share to 10 times that amount and recovered all its losses. Alas, the Emergency led to an economic recession and labour troubles resulted in a lockout, forcing Tata to rent apartments to complete orders and meet their clients' timelines. Eventually, Nelco ceased to exist in its original form and changed focus completely. Tata faced further challenges, such as setting up a flying club in Jamshedpur at J.R.D.'s behest and the time he spent at Empress Mills—till date he regrets the Group's decision to withhold the investment that could've saved the company. He later realized that these were all perhaps tests that J.R.D. had set.

Tata completed a management programme at Harvard Business School in 1975 and became chairman of Tata Industries in 1981. To the chagrin of many in senior positions, he was named J.R.D.'s successor a decade later to lead the organization into an era of economic liberalization. He proved his detractors wrong by pushing India to become a globalized nation with the purchase of foreign brands such as Tetley and Jaguar Land Rover. He converged the separate companies under the Tata brand, thus uplifting their individual worth and establishing the brand's presence in almost every sphere of our lives—food, housing, commerce, transport, communication—you name it. Under his leadership, net profit grew 50 times. Despite having headed one of the world's largest organizations for over two decades, Tata remains off the lists of the wealthiest people. This is because two-thirds of the Group is held by philanthropic trusts that work in areas of healthcare, rural upliftment, urban poverty alleviation, education and innovation, among others—staying true to the Tata legacy of helping India's economy grow to aid social welfare.

LASTING LESSON

We tend to reduce the purview of accomplishments by measuring them in money. While gauging advancements in someone's career, we look at how much they earn. We also concern ourselves with how much people around us spend—what car someone drives, what phone they use, what outfits they wear—thus attaching a price tag to everything and everyone. We don't limit this vision to others either; we internalize it and use it to view our own successes and failures. Except, careers aren't that straightforward. If we take up work for varied reasons including passion and the betterment of society, why should we measure how well we're faring with a singular statistic? It would be naïve to say that the importance of money should be entirely dismissed, but the definition of success needs to be broadened. As a leader of the business industry, Tata could have regarded profits as his major consideration and sold every single business that didn't make a splash in the bottom line, but there were many aspects to consider—what those companies' significance would be in the long term, how important those industries were to the country, how shutting them down would impact employees' lives. Though Tata is counted among the greatest living business minds by *Forbes*, he is nowhere near their wealthiest list. It is said that if he solely cared for personal wealth generation, he would have easily joined the billionaire club. One of the major reasons the Tata brand elicits trust in the consumer is because it is associated with high ethics and goodwill. While funds are required to access not just necessities but luxury items that can bring us joy, they shouldn't be the one and only marker of our feats as:

PROSPERITY DOES NOT EQUAL SUCCESS.

Tata's Tail-waggers

Fond of dogs, Tata relaxes by spending time with his two German shepherds. But his love for canines isn't restricted to foreign breeds. Years ago, he allowed strays to take shelter inside his offices during rains and allocated leftovers from the Taj kitchens for the dogs too. In 2018, a restoration of Bombay House, the Tata Group's head office, included the building of a full-fledged dog kennel with sleeping, playing and feeding areas.

BE KIND TO THE SELF

Lady Gaga (b. 1986)

Musician

Let's work together to beckon the world towards kindness.

Lady Gaga

Stefani Joanne Angelina Germanotta—or, as the world better knows her, Lady Gaga—has bagged every entertainment award that we can probably think of. The Oscar, Grammy, BAFTA, Golden Globe, Brit Award, VMA—you name it and she's won it, even setting a few Guinness World Records in the process. She wears numerous hats, those of singer, songwriter, actor, dancer, producer, director, philanthropist and fashion designer. But we first learnt of her as the trailblazing pop star with hits such as 'Bad Romance', 'Poker Face' and 'Born This Way'. Among the highest-paid women in music, her songs and videos are adored the world over. She has topped the charts in nations such as the United Kingdom, France, Germany, Finland, Russia, Australia, Canada and of course, her home country, the United States. Lovingly called 'Mother Monster' by her fans, she ranks among celebrities with the most Twitter followers as over 80 million people across the earth keep abreast of her every word. She has used her celebrity status and wide reach to speak up for equality and justice, so it's no wonder that she was named one of Elle's Women in Hollywood.

It's hard to imagine this global phenomenon as ever having failed, but Lady Gaga faced several hiccups in her career. Society failed her too and left marks on her psyche. The combined negative impact of all these elements reached a crescendo until her health came crashing down. The strength she showed in rising back up and proving the naysayers wrong is the reason why so many look up to her as a role model today.

THE WOMAN UNDERNEATH THE COSTUME

Lady Gaga was born as Stefani Germanotta on 28 March 1986 in New York City, US, to a family of Italian descent. Her father Joseph, an Internet entrepreneur, and mother Cynthia, a business executive, come from humble roots but brought up their two daughters in the more lavish Upper West Side of Manhattan. Germanotta showed an inclination towards music at an early age and began playing the piano by ear at age four. Her mother asked her if she wanted to take lessons, which confused the child because she said that she heard the music in her head—she didn't understand why she would need lessons for that. She did, however, become a classically trained pianist and wrote her first ballad by age 13.

Germanotta stood out from her peers at school, a trait that adults usually aspire to but children can get mercilessly teased for. Her school locker was vandalized with slurs. She was even thrown into a trash can and pointed and laughed at as a 'joke' by kids her age because she didn't fit the mould. Unlike her wealthy classmates, she worked as a waitress at a diner after school. She continued developing her musical skills and studied method acting for close to 10 years. Owing to her innate talent and the work she put in, a 17-year-old Germanotta gained early admission to a music programme at Tisch School of the Arts, New York University. While she expanded her knowledge there, she felt she needed to experience the real life of a working musician by playing at venues, so she dropped out after one year. Her father gave her the deadline of a year to make something of herself, or she would have to rejoin college.

In 2005, Germanotta formed the Stefani Germanotta Band or the SGBand, which played gigs in New York. A week before the cut-off date set by her father, she was scouted at one of her performances, which brought her to the attention of a music producer. Together, they recorded tracks and sent them to music industry executives. This initiative got her signed by a record label that year, but sadly they dropped her a few months later. It was at this point that she discovered the neo-burlesque scene. She met performance artist Lady Starlight, and the two formed their own go-go dancing variety act. Through it, Germanotta honed her performance skills and onstage persona. Her friends had been calling her 'Gaga' for some time by then, after the Queen song 'Radio Ga Ga', and she reportedly took on the 'Lady' in honour of her friend Lady Starlight, thus birthing the Lady Gaga we know. She served a songwriting apprenticeship at Famous Music Publishing and received a music publishing deal with Sony/ATV when it acquired the former. This opportunity gave her the chance to write songs for popular singers and groups such as Britney Spears, Fergie and The Pussycat Dolls. Gaga finally got her own record deal with an imprint of Interscope in late 2007. Despite it, radio stations refused to play her songs because they thought her music wasn't mainstream enough. Confident in her sound, the young artist said in response that she was the next big thing—and boy, was she right.

Releasing her debut album *The Fame* in August 2008, Gaga topped charts across the globe. She set up her own creative team, Haus of Gaga, which executes her costumes, make-up and stage sets on the basis of her ideas. Although she started out as an opening act for New Kids on the Block in 2008 and The Pussycat Dolls in early 2009, it wasn't long before Gaga headlined her own world tours. The Fame Ball Tour ran from March to September of 2009. While travelling, she wrote eight new tracks that formed *The Fame Monster* EP, which was released in November that year and even featured a song in collaboration with one of the music industry's superstars, Beyoncé. The success of the two albums allowed Gaga to head out on a second world tour and release *The Remix*. Lady Gaga became a worldwide phenomenon, famous for her dance music and shocking performances that delivered socio-political commentaries as well as costumes like the notorious 'meat dress'—an outfit made entirely of raw meat that she wore to the 2010 MTV Video Music Awards (VMAs).

Gaga's subsequent album was also successful—the title track of *Born This Way* had over a million downloads on iTunes in five days, earning her a Guinness World Record. In April 2012, she embarked on another world tour, The Born This Way Ball, with dates lined up in six continents.

However, on 13 February 2013, Gaga announced she was cancelling the remaining dates of the tour. Her body had finally reached its limit by being put through constant stress. After keeping her pain secret for a few months as she practised and performed intricate dance routines, she could barely walk. She thought she had injured her muscle, but upon reaching the hospital she found that she had broken her right hip and suffered a massive joint tear. What's more, the surgeons told her that had she ignored her pain any longer and performed even one more show, she might've needed a full hip replacement with convalescence for a whole year—all this before she turned 30. As a perfectionist who had been performing from her teen years, Lady Gaga was used to overworking herself at the expense of her physical and mental well-being. Following the surgery, a crossroads presented itself to her that would determine how she balanced her ambitions with her health:

Path 1
As soon as she got the all-clear from the doctors, Gaga could continue to follow the pace she had been used to for over a decade. There was a creative force inside her that must be sated, and she needed to oversee every aspect of her career to ensure it stood up to her high standards. She had to work on another album—her fans were waiting, restless, especially after the cancelled tour dates, so she had to deliver. She'd built up the persona of an unattainable celebrity, and pain is so... *human*. So *normal*. Whereas, *the* Lady Gaga was most definitely not.

Path 2

The stage persona Germanotta had created of Lady Gaga was a part of her that had been waiting to be unleashed, but it wasn't just a character. Lady Gaga was human, and her vulnerabilities were what made her relatable to her fans. She could take the time to get better and use music as a way to alleviate her pain and anxiety, instead of perceiving it as a task to be ticked off on her checklist. Hadn't she been speaking about love and compassion through her music? Shouldn't she extend that to her own self? Perhaps she could use her platform to talk about issues that are usually ignored, such as physical pain and mental health.

While the refunds of 200,000 ticket sales from the cancelled dates reportedly cost the tour $25 million, the incident also unfortunately left a serious injury that would trouble Gaga for years to come. She began opening up about not only her physical health, but also her mental health issues and how the two were intertwined. At age 19, Gaga was sexually assaulted by a man at a senior position in the entertainment industry, and she didn't speak about it to anyone for years. When she finally confessed to powerful men in the industry—people she looked up to—they proved unhelpful in getting her justice. Neither did they provide her the guidance she required to address the resulting mental illness. She was later diagnosed with post-traumatic stress disorder (PTSD) and fibromyalgia, which sends her body into spasms, making it hard for her to breathe at times. Due to these issues, she suffers from widespread chronic pain, which would be debilitating for anyone, but especially a performer. Furthermore, being bullied at school, assaulted in her industry and told multiple times that she would never amount to anything scarred her self-esteem and made her doubt herself at every turn.

Though fibromyalgia has no cure, Gaga receives treatment for it while her career soars to heights perhaps even her most ardent fans couldn't have imagined. Since recovering from her surgery, she has experimented with new genres and released more albums—*Artpop*, *Cheek to Cheek* (in collaboration with iconic jazz musician Tony Bennett), *Joanne*, as well as the soon-to-be released *Chromatica*.

She also starred in a season of the TV show *American Horror Story* and as the leading actor in the Hollywood movie *A Star Is Born* alongside Bradley Cooper. Her acting chops in the film scored her nominations at the Oscars, BAFTA, Golden Globes and Screen Actors Guild Awards, and the film's lead single 'Shallow' earned her numerous honours, including an Oscar and a Grammy. In spite of all these career-related accomplishments, Gaga says that her most cherished achievement is the 2012 launch of her and her mother's passion project, the Born This Way Foundation, a non-profit focused on youth empowerment.

LASTING LESSON

We should forge compassion for others, but we also need to be kind to our own bodies and minds. The tired cliché of the 'rat race' is often used to describe life, and as the population and the competition grow, it sadly gets truer every day. University admission cut-offs increase each year to impossible numbers, as do our expectations from ourselves or our children. Politics and competition at work leave us haggard as we tirelessly chase the *next*—the next project, the next bonus, the next promotion. Even something as common as our daily commute becomes stressful because we're always in a rush—a rush to be faster and better than our peers or our past selves. In doing so, however, we put ourselves under immense pressure, treating our bodies like machines that can never break down. But machines do break down, and so do we. We're organic matter, and while we have the ability to grow and repair, we need time and rest. There is no point in wearing blinders and speeding through life, only to fall apart midway. We can incorporate small changes that will have a long-term impact. We can exercise and meditate to keep our bodies fit and reduce stress, but we have to learn to ask for help too. It is possible to be strong and independent while recognizing we can't do everything and sometimes need care. Showing vulnerability is not equivalent to being helpless or 'pathetic.' This may be easier said than done, especially when it comes to mental health. The brain is an organ and needs tending to, and sometimes it gets sick and needs doctors and prescribed medication. The extreme standards we hold ourselves to should be shattered, and we have to allow us the downtime to repair and recuperate as we learn to:

BE KIND TO THE SELF.

Gaga's Genus

In 2012, a newly discovered genus of ferns was named after Lady Gaga. The ferns in question have fluid definitions of gender at a stage of their lives, harking to the way Lady Gaga challenges gender norms (in fact, she even performed as a male alter ego named Jo Calderone at the 2011 MTV VMAs). The ferns also have a distinct DNA sequence that spells out 'GAGA'. One species was called 'Gaga germanotta' to honour her family, and another was labelled 'Gaga monstraparva', the latter word literally meaning 'monster-little' for Lady Gaga's fans, whom Mother Monster affectionately calls her 'little monsters'.

LASTING LESSONS RECAP

1. Struggles are inevitable

2. Adapt, or become irrelevant

3. We are not our circumstances

4. How we play counts more than winning

5. Say yes to smart risks

6. Find joy in work

7. Nothing can replace hard work and perseverance

8. Do not fear failure

9. No work is small work

10. Success requires sacrifice

11. It's never too late

12. Challenges reveal our best selves

13. Focus on the big picture

14. Harness every teammate's strength

15. Choose inspiration over comparison

16. Remain flexible for reinvention

17. Critics aren't always right

18. Master trades relevant to the job

19. More than one route leads to triumph

20. Prosperity does not equal success

21. Be kind to the self

ACKNOWLEDGEMENTS

We all crave to trace an overall design in the way our lives unfold, and I will attempt to do so here in reverse chronological order. I cannot begin without thanking Rupa Publications for this opportunity and Team Rupa for believing I could tackle such a fascinating but expansive topic. I received this book offer while I was awaiting the result of my MSc Creative Writing degree, and I will forever be grateful to my professors at The University of Edinburgh for developing and shaping my craft—Claire Askew, Robert Alan Jamieson, Jane McKie, Michelle Keown, Allyson Stack and Valentina Bold. While I have been writing from the age of eight, I began to sincerely pursue it during my undergraduate days, and the first teachers to recognize and encourage my potential were the lovely Madhu Grover, Rukshana Shroff, Kasturi Kanthan and Shernaz Cama at Lady Shri Ram College for Women.

I am fortunate to be surrounded by friends who enjoy books, wish the best for me and never hesitate in calling me out. For your valuable guidance, thank you Shantanu Duttagupta and Daniel Ryan Adler. Kalyani Gandhi, Sucharita Das, Vandita Rohidekar and Lis Mesa, I couldn't have done this without your support whenever the imposter syndrome reared its monstrous head and told me I would fail. And Cephla—your dogged persistence in ensuring I stuck to my writing schedule was annoying and much appreciated.

The next trio deserves their own paragraph (and much more). My parents, Alka and Rajan Misra, and my brother Kartik—you enabled me to follow paths that instinctively felt right to me, though they might have seemed absurd or frivolous to the world. People I grew up with have become successful at more conventional jobs, yet no one jumps higher, screeches louder or hugs harder than you three whenever I thrive in my alternative line. Thank you for being wonderfully and oddly you and undoing the stereotype of the middle-class family.

And lastly, for providing me company in the late nights of researching and writing, I'd like to mention my adorable dog Rico in the hope that one day he'll learn to read in order to spot his name here.

Printed in Great Britain
by Amazon